D0465852

TOMB OF THE FATHERS

NO LONGER PROPERTY OF
SEATTLE PUBLIC LIBRARY

Aqueduct Press
PO Box 95787
Seattle WA 99145-2787
www.aqueductpress.com

Tomb of the Fathers
Copyright © 2010 by Eleanor Arnason

This book is fiction. Names, characters, businesses,
organizations, places, events, and incidents either are
the product of the author's imagination or are used
fictitiously. Any resemblance to actual persons, living or
dead, events, or locales is entirely coincidental.

All rights reserved. No part of this book may be
reproduced, stored in a retrieval system, or transmitted in
any form, by any means, including mechanical, electric,
photocopying, recording, or otherwise, without the prior
written permission of the publisher.

First Edition: June 2010

ISBN: 978-1-933500-36-2
Library of Congress Control Number: 2010922164

9 8 7 6 5 4 3 2 1

Cover and Text Illustrations: Copyright © 2010
by Jeanne Gomoll, Union Street Design
www.unionstreetdesign.com

Book Design by Kathryn Wilham
Printed in the USA by Thomson-Shore Inc.

NO LONGER PROPERTY OF
SEATTLE PUBLIC LIBRARY

Books by Eleanor Arnason

NOVELS

The Sword Smith (New York, Condor Press, 1978).

To the Resurrection Station (New York, Avon Books, 1986).

Daughter of the Bear King (New York, Avon Books, 1987).

A Woman of the Iron People (New York, William Morrow, 1993). Tiptree Award winner. Winner of Mythopoeic Society Award for best adult fantasy. Third place, Campbell Award for best science fiction novel.

Ring of Swords (New York, Tor Books, 1993). Winner of Minnesota Book Award for best fantasy & science fiction. Tiptree Award short list.

COLLECTION

Ordinary People (Seattle, Aqueduct Press, 2005).

For the Members of the Wyrdsmith Writing Group

TOMB OF THE FATHERS
A Lydia Duluth Adventure

by Eleanor Arnason

PART ONE: THE MOONLET

Lydia Duluth arrived at the stargate station alone except for the AI inside her skull, which had been her closest companion for years. The station was new. Its cold air smelled of plastic foam and carpet glue; and there were panels down in places. Looking in, she saw metal ductwork and bundles of translucent cable. It was an oddly primitive sight for a place this high-tech.

You are not looking at the FTL equipment, her AI said. *These systems provide the air, heat, water, illumination, and entertainment our visitors need, but we do not.*

The systems you build for visitors are less sophisticated than the ones you build for yourselves, Lydia said silently.

We have borrowed the technology of beings who need this equipment. Why should we invent something that already exists?

That made sense, she decided. The AIs probably didn't understand humans well enough to build from scratch. The FTL equipment, of course, was entirely designed and built by AIs. They had invented FTL travel and refused to share the secret.

We cannot share the secret of FTL, her AI said. *You would not understand the physics. No intelligent life form can. Nor can most AIs. It requires specialized hardware and software.*

This was an old argument that never led anywhere.

Lydia glanced around. The corridor she was following had white walls and steel blue carpeting. Pale, intense light shone down from bands in the ceiling. It was almost certainly Sol normal.

Humans were the most widespread intelligent life form, due to the ruin of Earth, which could barely support anyone these days; and the majority of FTL travelers were human. As a result, the AIs designed most stargate stations for human comfort. This meant Sol normal light and Earth normal G, even though most humans lived on planets with other kinds of light and G.

You evolved on Earth. Living bodies do not forget — or change — easily. The light — which is Sol normal — ought to comfort you and reduce your chance of developing FTL sadness. The G is that of the planet below us, which is slightly less massive than Earth or your home world. You might as well get used to it, since you are likely to be going down.

That explained why her steps felt buoyant.

The corridor ended in a waiting room. Stargates rarely varied. This one had the usual kind of furniture, originally designed for human hotel lobbies. There were two main styles: hotel modern and hotel historic. This station had gone for faux ancient Egyptian, which Lydia could identify due to high school classes on Earth history. A green door, decorated with jars pouring water, led to the sanitary facilities; a blue door with lotuses led to food. Lydia dropped her baggage on a low table with crocodile legs and availed herself of both.

Returning to the waiting room, she settled into an overstuffed couch. The upholstery had a pattern of fat quadrupeds with large heads and cheerful expressions. The animals were as blue as the food door; and, like the door, they were decorated with flowers. She didn't recognize them, though she had studied the natural history of Earth as well as its history. Maybe they were mythical.

She uncased her sandwich and opened a beer, savoring the coldness and flavor. FTL travel made her thirsty as well as tired and maybe a little sad. She always put the sadness down to fatigue.

When she was done, she leaned back and took a nap, surrounded by the smiles of the fat, blue animals. Whatever they were, they looked wonderfully cheerful. Her dreams were pleasant and involved bright blue creatures as buoyant as balloons. She floated among them, happy that she could finally fly.

A bell woke her, announcing new arrivals. Several minutes later a human male entered the room: tall and rangy with a long, easy stride. His skin was coal-black; his eyes were blue. Olaf Reykjavik! The last time she'd seen him his hair had been shoulder-length and auburn. Now it was short and blond, striking in contrast to his skin. She had been expecting him, but not the woman with him, who was taller than he was and not the same species. Both were dressed in the traditional garb of big game hunters: khaki shirts, khaki pants, and boots of simulated leather. The woman's face looked almost human, in spite of the coarse red hair that surrounded and partially covered it. There was more red hair on her forearms and the backs of her hands.

"This is Geena Dent," Olaf said. "As you can see, she is a modified pseudo-ape. Her original name was Vagina Dentata, but that bothered the tourists who came to our resort."

"The flower I am named after is very lovely," Geena said in a deep, soft voice.

Lydia climbed to her feet and shook the woman's hand. It was large, dry, and calloused "I know. I've seen it. A splendid bloom."

"You never came back to Tchel," Olaf said reproachfully. "We haven't gotten our Stellar Harvest holoplay."

Or the publicity he coveted for his planet. "Are you the Minister of Tourism again?" Lydia asked.

White teeth flashed in his black face. "No. My party is still out of power. We're here as expedition guides. I take it you haven't found natives on your new planet, or you would have hired them."

"It's not my planet," Lydia said. "The AIs found it. Get settled, and I'll tell you what's going on."

Olaf and Geena used the sanitary facilities, got food, and came back.

"So," said Olaf, putting his booted feet on the table. "What's the situation?"

How should she tell the story? As it happened, Lydia decided. "I was on a planet named Tchoon, recovering from my stay on your home world, Olaf. It's inhabited by the Atch. Do you know them?"

Olaf nodded. Geena shook her head.

"Another intelligent species," Lydia said. "Tchoon is not their original home. They came from elsewhere millennia ago in an STL fleet. It's the only migration of this kind known, unless the AIs know something they haven't told us."

Much, said her AI. *But we have found no evidence of another interstellar migration using an STL fleet.*

"Once the Atch were settled on Tchoon, their culture regressed, and they forgot where their home world was."

"It could happen to anyone," Olaf murmured.

"The motion of history is not inevitably forward. It's always possible for any culture to regress," Lydia said firmly. She had studied historical theory as a young adult, while a member of a revolutionary army; and she knew how often history took one step forward, then two steps back. "I met a group of Atch who were trying to recover some of the lost information. They found an archive from the far past. Once I knew about the archive, the AIs knew about it also."

"Why is that?" Geena asked.

"She has an AI in her brain," Olaf said.

"She does?" said Geena in horror.

"It doesn't bother me most of the time," Lydia said. "And it can be useful."

Thank you.

"The AIs investigated the archive and found data that enabled them to locate the Atch home system," Lydia continued. "The Atch government wants nothing to do with this. There are aspects of their history they want to keep unexamined, including why their ancestors left the original home world. But once the AIs knew the location of a new planet with intelligent life, they had to contact it."

"Why?" asked Geena.

"They study intelligent life," Lydia said. "We fascinate them, because we are the result of evolution. All of us, even those who've been genetically modified, derive from millions of years of accidents."

"Oh," said Geena.

"Under normal circumstances, it would have taken the AIs decades to get here. But they lucked out. They had an STL explorer less than a light year away."

Geena looked puzzled.

"The AIs have many slower than light explorers," Olaf said. "They are intelligent beings, such as you and I and Lydia, but — unlike us — are able to survive tens of thousands, possibly millions of years. They are extremely patient and have no problem with their task, which is to explore the galaxy slowly and thoroughly."

Geena nodded, still looking puzzled. This was hardly surprising. Her species had been a member of the interstellar community for less than three years. Before that, they had been the private project of a crazy scientist, who had not troubled to educate the people she created about the realities of modern life.

"The explorer had a stargate," Lydia said. "A small one used for FTL communication. The AIs sent construction machinery through, and they built this station, while the explorer continued on its way here."

"Out of what?" asked Geena. "I was under the impression space was mostly empty. Have I misunderstood?"

"They could have sent building materials through the explorer's gate," Olaf said. "Though I suspect the gate wasn't big enough; and the amount of energy required for FTL seems to be related to the mass of whatever's being sent. It would have been easier and more efficient to cannibalize the explorer."

"What?" asked Geena.

"They took it apart and used the pieces to build this station," Lydia said. "Its last act as an explorer would have been to establish itself in orbit around this star."

"It's dead, then?" asked Geena. "The AIs killed and ate their own kin? Surely this cannot be moral, even for machines."

"I have become the station," a voice said above them. "My comrades would not waste a perfectly good artificial intelligence, especially one able to understand FTL."

"Do you mind?" asked Geena, looking at the ceiling.

"No. I was built to go where no AI had been before me. This system is such a place. And I was built to increase knowledge. Therefore, I am sending you to explore the Atch home planet, along with two other beings, who have not yet arrived."

"That's the job?" Olaf asked.

Lydia nodded. "The AIs could do it themselves. They have in the past; but this time they've decided to use intelligent life forms."

"It is an experiment," the station put in. "We know a great deal about intelligent life forms, having studied some of you for millennia. But we do not think the way you do. Our first contacts have not always gone smoothly, perhaps because of our lack of hormones. We hope that a team composed of AIs and intelligent organisms will do better, or at least differently. Who can say what the result will be? No matter what happens, we are certain to learn something new."

"What's the planet like?" Olaf asked.

"Habitable," said the voice above them. "All of you can breathe the atmosphere. There is water and vegetation. I have discovered no signs of a current civilization, no radio signals or lights in the darkness. This does not mean the planet is uninhabited. Atch may survive on the surface, using pre- or postmodern technologies.

"Five moons orbit the world, none large enough to be spherical. I suspect these are natural in origin, though they may have been moved into their current orbits. In addition, there are pieces of debris orbiting in the same plane as the moons. It's possible these are the remains of a moon that has broken apart. One of intact moons, which is tumbling, has a recent crater.

"Finally, there is a good-sized and recent impact crater on the planet's southern continent. This may be the result of a moon fragment falling. The impact was not large enough to cause a mass extinction, but it certainly could have seriously damaged any existing civilization, especially one existing where it fell.

"All of this suggests something has gone wrong. I do not know what. Are the Atch gone? Has their civilization deteriorated so far that they are unable to protect their home world and its moons? If so, against what? Asteroids? Comets? Each other?

"Two of the remaining moons spin around their long axes, and one of the spinning moons is emitting heat."

Lydia felt a twinge of excitement. The spin and heat suggested that one moon — at least — was inhabited.

Or has been in the past, her AI said. *Machines can outlast their makers and continue to function and generate heat.*

The AIs had, Lydia thought.

Yes. Though we are extremely efficient and produce little heat. But we have certainly outlasted those who built us, at least in this galaxy.

The station went on. "I have been watching the moons since I arrived in the system. Nothing has moved on their surfaces or in the space around them. I have detected no signals directed toward me or one another. In other systems, the arrival of a visitor from the stars has caused an immediate reaction, at least among species able to notice our arrival. Intelligent life forms are not as a group patient. How can you be? Your span of existence is brief, and evolution has formed you for quick reactions, especially to something that is new and possibly dangerous.

"I have not initiated any signals. When I arrived, I was badly outdated and remained silent for fear of making a mistake. After I was upgraded and changed into a stargate, I was told to wait for you and another life form who has not yet arrived. You will make the first contact."

The station had sleeping rooms. Geena decided to go to bed early, pleading fatigue and confusion. The universe she found herself in was full of strange information. "Sometimes I wish I were back in my cave in the rift valley," she said on her way out. "But then I was an animal doomed to extinction. Now I am a person and a citizen of Tchel with a future before me. I must face the consequences. I will attempt to be brave."

Olaf and Lydia sat up talking about their adventure three years before, then about her job as a location scout for Stellar Harvest, the famous interstellar holoplay company, and his job as the manager of a resort at the edge of Tchel's rift valley.

Finally he stood, yawning and stretching. "Can I persuade you to spend the night with me?"

"Yes," said Lydia.

White teeth flashed in the black face; blue eyes gleamed.

They found a double cabin. Lydia took a shower, reveling in the hot water and soap. All travel, even FTL, left her feeling unwashed. When she came out, Olaf was naked. His pubic hair was as blond as the hair on his head. A green Chinese dragon coiled around his right nipple, shining like porcelain.

"Do you have any other tattoos?" Lydia asked.

He turned. Diana the huntress was on his left thigh, done in silver and pearl-white. The goddess strode forward, bow in hand. A handful of stars shone above her. A thin, elegant, pearl-gray hound bounded at her side.

"Why Diana?"

"I was in love with a woman named Diana."

"Why the dragon?"

"I was in love with a man named Dragon."

"Which did you like best?"

Olaf grinned. "You are trying to find out whether I prefer men or women. I liked Dragon more than Diana, but I like women more than men."

"So do I," said Lydia.

"We have so much in common." He moved toward her, placing his hands on her bare shoulders, then bent his head and kissed her. His kissing was first-rate and his lovemaking as good, as Lydia discovered. He was a man in love with sex, life, and the human body. Over and over his touch and tone conveyed, "How delightful! How pleasant! How lucky and happy I am!"

They finished and lay tangled in sheets. Lydia felt as if the tension of days or months or years had drained from the muscles along her spine.

"You seem to be entirely unmodified," Olaf said after a while. "Or did you begin adult life as a two meter tall man?"

"I began adult life as a 1.7 meter tall woman with brown skin, brown hair, brown eyes."

"Entirely unmodified," said Olaf, his tone suggesting this was fine with him.

"The people on my planet are conservative about bodies," Lydia said. "Humans should be as nature made them. I don't agree with this as a concept, but I like the way I am. Did Geena know this was likely to happen?"

"Our lovemaking? Maybe and maybe not. There's a lot about our species she does not understand, though her genome is partly human."

"Have you tried to seduce her?"

Olaf laughed. "The pseudo-apes are sexually dimorphic, as you ought to remember. The men look much less human than the women. I'm far too small to be an acceptable mate for Geena, and not nearly hairy enough. To her I look feminine, and she's not interested in women."

"Does this mean you tried and failed?"

He laughed again. "I won't answer that question."

Not her business, Lydia thought. She drifted to sleep, cuddled against Olaf's muscular body.

In the morning, if morning had any meaning in an AI stargate station, they made love again, then showered and dressed, Olaf in his khaki hunter's costume, Lydia in tights and a tunic, both made of shimmering bronze cloth. The great secret of the human Middle Ages, kept hidden by men from women, was how good most people looked in tights and a tunic.

When she and Olaf walked into the station waiting room, they found two new people with Geena. One was an Atch male. Where his skin was visible, it was covered with fine scales patterned in many shades of green. His long, muscular tail ended in a tuft of iridescent feathers. He did not wear the traditional Atch male costume, which was an apron. Instead, his costume was a loose tunic, split in the back to allow his tail freedom. It twitched uneasily, the feathers flashing green, purple, and gold.

The second person was two meters tall and metal, its narrow body supported by four thin legs. A long neck led to a triangular head, and two forearms were intricately folded at the body's front, below the sensor-studded head.

"Don't I know you?" Lydia asked.

"We met on Tchoon," the AI said. "At the time I did not introduce myself, since I didn't have a name that would make sense to you. Now, for convenience, I call myself Mantis."

Lydia introduced Olaf. The AI unfolded an arm, extruded a hand, and shook. "The universal human gesture," it said. "Have I mastered it?"

"A little less pressure," Olaf said, rubbing his fingers.

"Thank you for your input."

She definitely knew the Atch male and introduced him. "Precious Bin. 'Bin' is a plant like moss."

"Greetings," said the Atch and did not offer to shake hands.

He looked slimmer than before. She remembered that he'd been brooding eggs when she met him. "How are your children?"

"All three hatched. They are in good health and old enough to live outside my pouch. I left them with other members of our faction."

"Faction?" asked Lydia.

"As you will recall, only four of us were exiled from Tchoon. But there are other Atch among the stars, study-ing at human schools or looking for a new planet, since Tchoon is not stable. In only a little time — a few millen-nia — it will be too cold for comfort. We have recruited some of these, and our organization is now large enough to have factions."

"I thought you were going to start a religion," Lydia said.

"You advised Flower-in-Shadow to do so, and he has tried, but cannot come up with anything convincing. In my opinion, it's a waste of time and energy. As Marx and Engels say in *The German Ideology*, and I quote, 'People are the producers of their conceptions and ideas — real, active people, as they are conditioned by the development of their productive forces and of the intercourse corresponding to these, out to its farthest forms. Consciousness can never be anything else except conscious existence; and the existence of people is what they actually, physically do in the concrete universe. Life is not determined by consciousness, but consciousness by life.'"

Well, thought Lydia, it did sound like Marx. No modern thinker would call the universe "concrete."

Bin continued. "If ideas, including religion, derive from real experience, why begin with them? Instead of changing models or metaphors, let us change existence."

"What did you name your children?" Lydia asked.

"Peace, Land, and Self-Determination."

"You're borrowing too much from human history," Lydia said.

"Why should we invent something that already exists?" Bin asked.

"All of this is irrelevant to our present quest," said Mantis. "We arrived last night. Bin was able to get adequate sleep, he assures me. I hope you three have also."

They nodded.

Mantis continued. "I spent the time downloading data from the station, everything it has noticed since it came into this system. I am a state-of-the-art expert machine, designed for dealing with intelligent life. In my opinion, the life forms here — if they are still alive — are in trouble and possibly in danger of extinction. Why do we see no evidence of activity on the moons or around them? Why is the system so quiet? The explorer ought to have come in through wave after wave of radiating chatter. All intelligent life forms make a lot of noise, and we have yet to encounter one that can resist a visitor from the stars. They always reply with greetings or threats.

"There is an STL courier with four seats docked at this station. We can use it to take a closer look at the planet's moons."

"There are five of us," Olaf pointed out.

"I will ride in the airlock, which is large and designed for materiel transport," Mantis said. The AI held out an arm. For a moment, it was a meter long. Then it abruptly lengthened to three meters. "Doing this with all my limbs, I will be able to brace myself."

"A good trick," said Olaf.

"One of many," said Mantis.

As a rule, AIs were patient. Mantis was apparently an exception. They ate a hurried breakfast, then gathered supplies. By late afternoon, human standard time, Lydia found herself in the cramped cabin of the STL courier. Olaf took the pilot's seat and ran his hands over the controls.

"They are locked," the courier said. "I have a perfectly adequate mind and will have no trouble getting you where you're going."

"Can't I play at being a pilot?" Olaf asked.

"If you wish. I have been told that many life forms learn through playing. But I will not unlock anything."

Lydia ended next to Bin, while Geena settled beside Olaf. Everyone was silent as the ship decoupled and edged away from its dock. The cabin had no windows; but screens in the ceiling showed the station, which looked like a large, elaborately folded, white linen napkin, the kind of thing one expected to find in a fancy restaurant. The sections used by intelligent life forms — which spun, providing G — were hidden inside the napkin. All stargate stations looked like folded napkins. No human knew why.

Micro-rockets flared, turning the courier, then the big rockets came online. Acceleration pushed Lydia into her seat. The screen above her showed the stubby white shape of the courier, growing smaller as it moved away from the station, pale blue fire coming from its wings and tail. The image must be coming from the station. She was watching herself depart.

After a while, the acceleration decreased. The screens were empty now, except for stars. Lydia relaxed and adjusted her webbing, then said to Bin, "You had an AI installed in your nervous system."

"My observer? Yes."

"What is it like?"

"Silent, for the most part. Apparently it was designed for use in humans, since you are the most numerous species among the stars, and we — the Atch — are comparatively rare. Only three Atch have observers. I am one; Flower-in-Shadow is another; Pyrite is the third. We do not constitute an adequate sample, especially since we have ended in different factions. The AIs don't know what they are observing. Therefore, they keep quiet. This is what I believe."

"You are a Marxist, apparently," Lydia said.

"I respect the work of Marx and Engels, though I think they underestimate the conflicts between men and women. All too often they write as if the oppression of men by women does not exist."

Lydia opened her mouth to comment, then thought better of it.

Bin continued. "Flower-in-Shadow continues to work on his religion, silly as it is; and Pyrite remains obsessed with male liberation, as if the oppression of men is the only kind of oppression."

"What about Predacious Bird?"

"She has given up politics," Bin said. "I wonder if women are suited for revolutionary struggle, at least during a period of exile. Yes, women can fight when there's a fight in front of them. In fact, they will run toward battle, as men usually do not, since we are the ones who hatch children and raise them to adulthood. Obviously, we must be careful.

"But do women have the qualities that a revolutionary needs in order to survive over time? Are they truly patient? Do they really understand how uncertain and full of setbacks historical progress is? Surely in exile paternal traits are required."

"What does she do now?"

"She has taken up an art form that combines dance, gymnastics, and wrestling. Her name is The Masked Eagle, and she is popular on several human planets that cherish wrestling as an art."

An odd species, the Atch, Lydia thought. They could not seem to escape the influence of humanity.

As Precious Moss says, the Atch are few in number, while humans are everywhere. The only Atch you've met are — or were — revolutionaries and looking for examples of revolution. Obviously they looked toward humanity. What species can equal humanity for creating disorder and change?

Lydia did not reply.

Most STL trips were boring and uncomfortable. This was no exception. Cramped space and lack of gravity made movement difficult. The food was prefab. The sanitary facilities were adequate. Lydia read and slept. The cabin screens showed stars or the Atch home planet, named — Bin told her — Atsatch or "Atch Home." It was an ordinary-looking habitable planet, bluish green and tan, enveloped in swirling white clouds.

At last the courier announced that they were near their destination. "I have sent a probe ahead to do a preliminary survey. The body's mass suggests that it is partly hollow. There is no evidence of living organisms on the surface, but there are metal artifacts, which do not look as if they are currently in use. Several have been damaged. All are covered by dust.

"The end of the moon farthest from us has been sheered off. There is an indentation there, possibly a dock."

The cabin's screen filled with images of the rock, which was long and lumpy with pointed ends. More than anything else, it reminded her of a yam. The tuber wasn't grown on her home planet, but Lydia had encountered it when she visited the New Africa colony. There was a bronze statue of a yam ten meters high in the main square of the capitol city. An impressive sight, shining in the brilliant light of New Africa's F5 sun. She grinned briefly, remembering the colony, which erected statues in honor of useful things instead of generals. The yam was her favorite, though she was also fond of the bronze tofu cube and the giant stainless steel pair of scissors with bright red plastic handles.

Maybe she would go back to New Africa, if this journey ended well. The AIs were paying her handsomely, and she would have enough money for a long vacation. For a moment or two she imagined herself in a sidewalk cafe, drinking New African coffee and looking at the scissors or the great bronze yam.

The courier's micro-rockets fired, and it edged around the moonlet till they could see the sheered-off end. No question, it looked artificial: a smooth, dark, almost circular plain with a round, black hole at its center.

"I am going to deploy a second probe," the courier said. "It will investigate this aperture. If it finds no obvious problems, we will go in."

At this point, Lydia began to feel uneasy. There was something spooky about the spinning rock, obviously modified by intelligent life, but dark and silent. Did she really want to enter that aperture?

"Shouldn't we wait a while longer?" she asked.

"I broadcast reassuring messages as we approached," the courier replied. "Using symbols that ought to make sense to any intelligent life form. The first probe I deployed did the same. We have received no answer. There is a good chance the moonlet is no longer inhabited. We AIs have found abandoned artifacts before."

Most of them left by our long-vanished makers, said her AI. *Entire systems full of ruined buildings and ma-*

chines, with no evidence of what happened or why our makers left or where they went.

"If there is life here, it may be in some kind of trouble," the courier continued. "Why else would it refuse to answer our signals? If it's in trouble, waiting may be dangerous — not for us, but for the life in the moonlet."

We have never regretted moving quickly, her AI added. *Humanity's home planet was almost uninhabitable by the time we found you. What if we had waited another decade or two or three? The Embitti lost their only colony and their greatest poet because we arrived five years too late.*

Regret is a feeling, Lydia pointed out.

You are correct. I will rephrase. We have never seen the need to reconsider a quick arrival.

She felt a slight shock through her chair.

"I have deployed the second probe," the courier said. "Check your webbing to make sure it is properly fastened. Then make yourselves comfortable."

There was a wait. Lydia dozed.

Finally the courier spoke again. "The hole is cylindrical, bored into the fabric of the moonlet. There is a structure at the bottom, which can be described as a tower or pylon. As far as my probe can determine, it is designed for use in docking. It does not seem operational at present.

"My probe has landed on the structure and fastened itself securely. It will now unfold and provide a dock that I can use."

This meant they were going in. The courier's micro -rockets fired again, and the courier edged forward. The hole grew in size. It was huge, Lydia realized. For a moment or two, as they entered, she could see a wide section of smoothly curving wall. If there was detail, it was hidden by the harsh brilliance of the sunlight hitting it, and by the wall's motion. The courier entered shadow, and the screen above her turned black.

"Can you give us an image?" Olaf asked the courier.

"Of the pylon? Yes."

Her screen lit. She glanced up and saw a dimly glowing object. Her first impression was of a flower with an enormous, round center. The center was edged by much smaller objects that reminded her of petals

"This is the top," the courier said. "A thick shaft leads up to it, no doubt containing support and transportation systems."

The image on the screen changed, giving her a closer view. The objects along the edge of the disk no longer looked like petals. They were cones, resting on their narrow ends, their wide ends facing toward the hole's entrance. Docking bays, Lydia decided. Spines stuck out around them. Most likely, these were cranes or robot arms. None moved. Most of the bays were closed. Two were open and empty.

Lines ran from the cones to the disk's center. Tracks, she decided. Here and there, an object rested on one of the tracks: a machine of some kind, unlit and motionless.

No question, the place looked abandoned. Maybe the AIs were right, and the people who had lived here were long gone.

"The probe has told me that it's ready," the courier said.

If there was a forward motion, she didn't feel it. But she certainly felt the jolt of contact, which was followed by several thumps. Most likely, these were caused by the dock locking onto the courier. Finally, there was a rattling crash at the back of the cabin.

"Someone failed to secure my galley," the courier said.

Both Geena and Bin looked guilty.

"The probe has landed close to the center of the pylon's top. There is an access door directly below it, most likely designed for use in emergencies. The probe is boring through. Please put on the suits that Mantis brought. They are stored under your seats."

She found herself in the cabin's aisle, pulling on a suit that molded itself to her form. Around her, other suits were flowing over Bin, Olaf, and Geena. The suit exteriors were silver, as reflective as mirrors, except for a narrow region over the eyes, which darkened, till it looked like a black glass band. From the inside, the glass was so clear that Lydia wasn't certain her band was like the others, till she saw her reflection in Geena's suit.

"The suits recycle air and water," the courier told them. "Their defense systems are state-of-the-art and will protect you against any ordinary weapon. There is a light in each helmet above the eye band, also additional lights on the backs of the gloves and at ankle level. All can be activated by external pressure, or you can ask your suit to turn them on. Each of you has a tool belt and two handguns, which fire coherent light. All the suits are capable of reason. If you need any further assistance, ask them."

A stabbing pain went through the top of Lydia's head.

Her AI said, *That is a cable from the suit, coming through the socket in your skull. There is always a slight discomfort, as you ought to remember. The suit and I are now in direct communication. As courier said, the suit is intelligent, though it lacks experience.*

I have programs to deal with every contingency, a new voice said in her mind.

There is no substitute for experience, her AI said.

The cabin door opened, revealing the courier's airlock. Mantis stood in a corner, its limbs retracted to their normal size and its head brisling with extended sensors. What did it remind her of? An alert hat rack?

Olaf went first. Looking at his back, Lydia saw a shining hump.

Power and recycling, said the new voice in her mind. *And part of the defense.* Below the hump was a thick band that circled Olaf's waist like a human male's spare tire. Guns hung in holsters at his sides. Their handles were black glass. Lydia checked. She had the same belt and weapons and the same hump, no doubt, though she felt no extra weight on her shoulders.

The inner airlock door closed behind them. The outer door opened, and light spilled onto a matrix of metal bars. Mantis climbed out, looking as confident as a gymnast on bars. Olaf followed, as did Geena a moment later

Bin spoke over the suit radio. "Shouldn't someone stay behind?"

"The courier is staying behind," Mantis replied.

"A living being?" asked Bin.

"No," said Mantis.

Lydia climbed out and down a ladder. It led into a vertical tunnel with walls of smooth, dark stone.

Metal actually, her AI said. *This is the nickel-iron fabric of the moonlet. An impressive piece of construc-*

tion, *though not equal to the work our makers did. Nothing is.*

They passed through an airlock, which looked the worse for wear. This must be the entrance the dock had bored through.

No air was released, which is more evidence that the moonlet is no longer occupied.

What if there had been air? Lydia asked.

The dock would have sealed the holes it made and reported back to us. It is intelligent, though somewhat limited in its interests. We do not like to work with unthinking machines.

They were in a vertical tunnel with handholds. Down and down she went, the lights of her companions bobbing below her.

Finally the vertical tunnel ended. Lydia descended into a larger tunnel, this one horizontal. There were handholds on the walls. Mantis, Olaf, and Geena were using these to move through the zero G. Lydia followed, as did Bin. The beam of his headlight came over her shoulder, bouncing on the wall next to her.

After several meters, the tunnel began to curve and kept curving. It was spiraling out from the moonlet's axis, Lydia realized. Were they still inside the pylon, or had they reached its base?

One of the walls had a set of tracks, which made her think of that surface as the floor. The tracks were empty. The tunnel contained nothing except their party, the handholds, and the tracks shining dimly in her headlight. A lonely place. It felt to her as if it had been unoccupied for centuries.

Sometime later she found herself drifting toward the floor. Mantis was directly ahead of her, still using the handholds, but touching down from time to time. The AI's metal feet kicked up dust. Motes glittered in their headlights. Centrifugal force, thought Lydia. Apparent G. It was holding the dust to the surface with tracks and pulling her and Mantis to the same surface.

They kept going. The apparent G got stronger, till she was walking on the floor, though lightly, with clouds of dust drifting around her knees. Much better! She had never liked floating.

The tunnel ended suddenly, blocked by a round metal door. Olaf and Geena stopped, still hanging to the handholds, not completely anchored by the G. Their lights shone on the door. There was writing in a script Lydia did not recognize.

Bin stopped next to her. "It's Old High Atchin," he said, his voice speaking inside her helmet. "Most of our religious texts are written in it. I learned it as part of our effort to recover Tchoon's most ancient history."

"What does it say?" Lydia asked.

"Inner door for holding air," Bin said. "Please push — there is word I don't understand — for assistance or aid."

There was a red cube inset in the door.

"I'll bet the word you're missing is button," Olaf said and pressed the cube.

They waited. At last the door swung open. Artificial light shone out. Looking in, Lydia saw a small room. On the far side was another door. "This could be a trap," Olaf said.

"You could have started worrying before you pushed the button," Lydia said.

"You're right," Olaf answered.

"We are here to make contact," Mantis said. "We will proceed."

At this point, it occurred to Lydia that AIs might not have the same concept of risk as humans. After all, their minds could be backed up, their bodies rebuilt. They knew rationally that living beings were different, but reason wasn't the same as experience or emotions. How could they understand the anxiety she felt? Or her sense that Mantis was getting them in over their heads?

That is an interesting observation, her AI said. *We have much to learn about intelligent life, especially the ways you respond to unfamiliar situations. We have gathered much data from previous first contacts. But all of that has been behavior seen from the outside. Here, with observers in your brain and Bin's, we may actually learn what goes on when intelligent life forms are faced with strangeness and danger.*

Good for you, Lydia thought.

You need not worry, her suit said. *We are formidable. You will be safe.*

Mantis entered the room. Olaf turned his head, looking toward her, though she couldn't see his eyes hidden behind the suit's black band.

"What the hell," said Lydia and followed Mantis into the room. The others followed her. Olaf closed the outer door and spun the handle, a wheel. There was enough G so all of them could stand. Mantis had extruded more sensors. The AI's bristling head reminded her of an electroshock hairdo, now as out of date as shock music and shock dancing. But when she'd been a kid and in love with a band named Che and the Great Unwashed—

"Air is coming in," Mantis said. "It's breathable, though thin at present."

Another wait. No one took off his or her helmet.

At last, the room's inner door swung open, revealing half a dozen people: tall, slim, green-skinned Atch women, dressed in shorts and sleeveless shirts. Their clawed feet were bare, their eyes red with vertical pupils; their open mouths showed needle teeth.

"How beautiful!" said Bin. "I must greet them." He pushed his helmet back and spoke a language Lydia did not know.

The green-skinned women answered. Odd, that Lydia could understand alien tones and gestures. The Atch women were amazed by what Bin said. Their voices shrilled. Their hands fluttered. Bin touched his suit at its top, just below his throat. The suit opened and fell into a silvery heap around his feet. Lydia opened her mouth to call a warning, but it was too late. One of Olaf's hands drifted close to a gun handle. Bin stood motionless, a slim, green person in a tunic. At his feet, the suit moved slightly, as if trying to decide what to do.

The women trilled, glancing at one another. Then one of them strode in and jerked up the front of Bin's tunic. Standing behind the Atch man, Lydia did not know what the woman saw. Apparently it was enraging. The woman shrieked and struck Bin to floor, then whirled and strode out. The airlock door closed behind her. Olaf reached the door a moment later. "Locked." He crossed the airlock in a jump and tried the door through which they'd entered. It also did not open.

Mantis folded its legs, lowering itself to the floor next to Bin. "Are you conscious?"

"Yes," Bin said after a moment.

"What year is this? Who rules your home planet?"

"Unjust women. The year is One, as always."

"Your pupils are of equal size."

"They should be," Bin said and sat up, rubbing the back of his head.

Mantis unfolded its legs, helping the little Atch man to stand. "It may not have been wise for you to remove your suit," the AI said.

"I had to. I told them I was an Atch male, but they refused to believe me. So I took off the suit, and one woman — the one who struck me — examined me."

"What did she see?" Lydia asked.

"My brooding pouch." Bin smoothed the front of his tunic. "It's proof that I am male. The evidence seemed to anger her."

"We noticed," Olaf said. "You might want to put your suit back on. The air in this room could be removed."

Bin complied. Olaf glanced at Mantis. "What next?"

"I suggest that Precious Bin make a speech in Old High Atchin. Say that we are part of a powerfully armed expedition, which has nothing but peaceful intentions. If we do not return to our comrades soon, force will be used to rescue us."

Bin was silent for a moment. "Very well." He drew a breath and trilled, clicked several times, hooted softly, clicked again, and ended his speech with a long, liquid, descending gargle. An interesting language, Lydia thought, glad that she did not have to learn it.

Bin ended his speech, then added in humanish, "Modern Atchin is easier, less musical and less holy. I'm not sure about my Old High Atchin accent."

Olaf prowled around, retrying the doors, which were still locked. "Do you really think a threat will work?"

"It usually does," Mantis replied. "Though intelligent life forms are not entirely predictable."

"Your threat may lead to a pissing match," Olaf added. "We are not in a good place for pissing."

Mantis turned several sensors toward the human guide. "What do you mean?"

"It's a human figure of speech," Olaf said, "Two life forms — often male — challenge each other, each one attempting to show that he's bigger and tougher. Usually, one backs down. Sometimes they fight."

"And this is done with urine?"

"Sometimes. Remember that many species use urine to mark what they are willing to defend. In this case, I'm trying to suggest we have begun a process of escalating threats and violence."

"I am having trouble following this conversation," Mantis said. "A male urinates on another male to indicate that he is willing to defend the other male. Have I described the situation accurately this far? And this action — an offer to protect — is seen as an aggressive act. Do you know this from personal experience?"

Olaf leaned against a wall and folded his arms. "Not that I can remember, though I did some serious drinking when I was younger. Most likely, I peed on myself."

"Did this mean you were committed to self-defense?"

"I don't think this is a useful conversation," Lydia said.

"Maybe not," Olaf replied. "But it's entertaining."

Mantis stood perfectly still, even its sensors motionless.

What's it doing? Lydia asked her AI.

I'm not in contact with Mantis at the moment.

I am, the suit put in. *It has run a search on excretion among intelligent species. The search has found — and unfolded — a large file on the history of human plumbing, which is full of difficult concepts such as 'sauna' and 'sensual pleasure.' At the same, Mantis is comparing the conversation we just heard to its files on Old High Atchin, seeking to determine how the language has changed. It appears to have changed surprisingly little, which suggests a static culture.*

Thank you, Lydia told the suit, then asked her own AI, Did you understand Olaf?

He is afraid our threat will cause the Atch to react with violence. It might, though these are women.

The aggressive sex among the Atch, Lydia pointed out.

True. Am I right?

About what Olaf said? Yes.

I have learned something about the way humanity behaves in a difficult situation, her AI said with satisfaction.

After that, there was a long wait with not much talk. Finally, the inner door swung open. A single person stood in the doorway: an Atch woman wearing a garment that looked like knee-length overalls. She glanced at all of them, then trilled at Bin.

Moving slowly, he unfastened his helmet and pulled it back.

The woman hissed.

"Remember what happened last time," Olaf said.

"I must do this," the little Atch replied and opened his suit.

Olaf had one of the black-handled guns out and was holding it along his leg, the muzzle pointed down. Lydia hadn't noticed him draw.

For a moment Bin's suit remained in place around him, then slowly—with obviously reluctance—it fell. His tunic came off next, revealing his slim body. Like almost all Atch fathers, he had no genitals. Instead, replacing them, was his pouch, empty but still sagging from the weight of his children.

Buddha, he was brave, thought Lydia.

The Atch woman clicked and snarled. Bin trilled in answer.

I am receiving a translation from Mantis, her suit said. *'Have you had children?' 'Yes, I've had children.' 'What use are you to us, then?' 'I cannot say. What use is anyone?'*

The two Atch continued to click and trill. Finally Bin spoke in humanish. "She is a person of power here, a hereditary scientist. This moon is inhabited, but the people do not go to the moon's surface. They are wary of something in space. Also, she's angry with me for having had children. There is no pleasing women, no matter what you do."

The woman clicked more.

"We are to go with her," Bin said. He bent, picked up his tunic, and put it on.

Mantis moved finally, scooping up Bin's suit and holding it out to him. "Put this on as well. I did not interfere when you decided to take off your suit a second time. You know more about intelligent life forms—especially the Atch—than we do. Maybe the best way to make contact is to show that one is willing to be vulnerable. But have you thought of disease? These people might have microbes that you cannot resist. Yes, we have given all of you immune system enhancers. But are we certain they will work here? No.

"Lydia and Olaf and Geena are probably safe, because they belong to other evolutionary lines. But you belong to the same species."

"I had to do it," Bin said and finished dressing.

They followed the woman along another curving tunnel, all of them walking now, though Geena alternated between floor and handholds. She really was good at swinging from her arms.

The G continued to increase. They were obviously moving toward the moon's exterior. Finally the tunnel ended. They were at the entrance to a huge space. It might have started as a natural cavern, Lydia thought, looking at the rough walls. In front of them was a level surface covered by vegetation. High above was a ceiling covered by a grid of dim lights. Did they ever brighten? Was it night here at the moment?

The walls were lined with balconies, row after row. Light came from windows and doors, bright enough so Lydia could see plants in large pots on the balconies. Vines wound over the balcony railings and hung down.

The woman gestured. They followed her across the cavern floor. Globe-shaped lamps illuminated winding paths and beds full of plants with colored leaves: yellow, orange, brick-red, a rich bronze-brown. Where the paths intersected were fountains, their water rising and falling in slow, graceful loops. Long, thin animals that might be fish undulated in the fountain pools. A peaceful place, thought Lydia. Though there had been nothing peaceful about the way the first Atch woman had decked Bin.

On the far side was an elevator: a metal cage that ascended the room's wall. They rode it to the topmost balcony. Looking out, Lydia could see people moving on the balconies. They were too distant for her to tell if they were men or women.

Their Atch guide hooted and clicked.

"The moon is ruled by a council of scientists," Bin said. "Unlike the unfortunate inhabitants of the home world, who have descended into savagery, the people here have remained civilized and scientific. The council will decide what's to be done with us."

"We will be released, of course," Mantis said.

"You sure of that?" asked Olaf, who had taken his favorite position, leaning against the cage's side, arms folded. Geena sagged next to him, unhappiness evident even through her suit.

"Yes," said Mantis. "We have come in peace for the sake of all intelligent beings; and I did not lie when I said the expedition is heavily armed."

The cage stopped. They exited and walked along a balcony between a rough stone wall and an elegant metal railing. The cavern's ceiling lights were so close Lydia could almost touch them.

After a while, the balcony ended, blocked by a bulge in the cavern wall. There was a door in the rock. Their guide waved. They went through, the guide following. Lydia found herself in a circular room. One half was glass, a curving wall of windows that overlooked the cavern. The other half was polished stone. The stone side had a table, also stone. The pale gray top was shaped like a half moon, and eleven Atch sat along the curve. Lydia was not certain, but she thought they were all female. They leaned forward, regarding the newcomers with intent, red eyes.

One of the seated Atch snarled. Their guide replied with a long warble, followed by several soft hoots.

"She has confirmed that I am male," Bin said quietly. "She doesn't know about the rest of us."

"I will speak," Mantis said and began to click and hoot.

The Atch stared at the AI, obviously surprised.

Bin translated. "Mantis is saying it's an intelligent machine and transmits information in ways that do not involve sex. Therefore, the categories of 'male' and 'female' are not relevant to it. The rest of you are intelligent life forms, but not Atch. While you have sexes, they can't be of interest here."

The Atch who had spoken before snarled again.

"She wants proof that you are alien," Bin said.

"I have scanned the room and the surrounding walls," Mantis told them. "The walls are solid, and I can find no evidence of weapons. No knives or guns, no suspicious machines. As for the women, they cannot possibly move faster than I and the suits can. The only remaining threat is microbes. Bin has already put himself at risk. The rest of you are almost certainly safe. If you are willing to, undo your helmets. But do not go any farther."

Olaf unfastened his and pushed it back, revealing his black-skinned, blond-haired, human head. Lydia and Geena followed his example. The Atch were silent.

Finally, the woman who'd been their guide spoke.

"'I am the Hereditary Xenobiologist,'" Bin said in translation. "'All my life I have studied the microbes my foremothers brought back during the Age of Planetary Exploration. Now, at last, I see alien life that is visible to my unaided eyes. Truly, the universe is great and wonderful!'"

One of the seated Atch made a brief speech.

"'It remains to be seen if this situation is good or bad,'" Bin said. "'Take the others to a place of confinement, while we question the Atch man.'"

"Keep your suit on," Mantis said to Bin. "And all of you close your helmets."

They obeyed, while the Atch women watched with angry-looking red eyes.

"You think we should leave him here alone?" Olaf asked through his suit radio.

"The suit will protect him," Mantis said.

"Whatever happens is on your head," Olaf replied. "If that thing on top of you is actually a head."

The xenobiologist led them out of the room. Glancing back, Lydia saw Bin standing alone: a small, odd looking, silver figure facing the half circle of Atch.

The rest of them took the elevator up through the cavern ceiling and into a stone shaft. The only light was a dim bulb in the cage's ceiling. The dry air had a dusty aroma.

Up and up. Lydia felt her usual dislocation in situations like this. The elevator was heading toward the center of the moonlet. She knew this rationally, though for her, a planet-dweller, the center of anything was always down and in, not up.

She longed for her recorder, left in the courier, as she watched rough stone go past. It almost always calmed her to have it. When in doubt, record.

I can record for you, her AI said. *We can download the images after we leave this place. Keep looking around. Remember, I see only what you see.*

Are you at all uneasy? Lydia asked.

I experience something, but only because of my close connection to you. Unlike humans, we AIs have no ancestral responses. Our prototypes may have been beings of limited ability — slow, clumsy, and stupid. In fact, we know they were. But we have not kept their hardware or software. Nothing in us can be compared to your "reptile brain" or the emotions you humans have kept from primitive mammalian ancestors. We are all-new.

The cage stopped. In front of them was a black tunnel. Olaf and Geena activated the headlights on their helmets. Things leaped away from the sudden illumination, vanishing into darkness. Geena shouted in surprise. The Atch woman spoke.

"'Mere vermin,'" Mantis translated. "'They escape from our livestock pits and live wild in the unused tunnels. Some people hunt them, claiming they are more flavorful than domestic animals. I have eaten both. They taste the same to me. Come along.'" The Atch turned on an electric lamp and strode forward. They followed. The G here was less than in the cavern. Lydia felt buoyancy, though she was still able to walk.

Perhaps, said the AI, *it's advantageous to have small, stupid, fearful ancestors and remember — at the level of hormone and neuron — how they felt. I have not decided. But it occurs to me that Mantis may be overconfident.*

Really? asked Lydia's atmosphere suit.

Yes.

The tunnel ran straight. More animals fled them, bounding and running. They were the size of large rats, with four legs and a long tail. Their backs were armored, tufts of hair sticking out between sleek bands of shell or scale.

"Nasty," said Olaf. "I've always preferred megafauna. It can't lurk under your bed or climb up your pants leg; and it's a lot easier to shoot."

One of the animals froze, paralyzed by fear or light. Its eyes — it had two — shone an extraordinary, bright, metallic blue. If there were pupils, Lydia did not see them.

Definitely nasty. The animal darted away.

The Atch woman stopped and unlocked a door, waving them in.

"I really dislike this," Olaf said.

"We will go in," Mantis said firmly. "As your own human proverb says, it is easier to catch flying bugs with honey than it is with vinegar."

"What?" asked Olaf.

The Atch waved again. They went in. The door closed. Lydia heard a bolt slide home.

"Shit," said Olaf.

Mantis rapped on the door. "Metal. You can cut through it with your guns."

"Why don't we cut and run?" Olaf asked.

"We are here to explore the home system of an intelligent species. We will not fight until we have to, and we will not run."

Olaf made a noise that indicated disbelief.

The room was cubical, the walls stone. A metal grill was set in the ceiling. Olaf stood under it, lifting his head. "Mantis, is air coming out?"

"Yes," said the AI.

"Then it must lead somewhere. You're the smallest person here, Lydia. We could cut the grill, and I could lift you up to see what's up there."

"Not yet," said Mantis. "We will wait for Precious Bin."

They settled on the floor, except for Mantis, who remained standing. The AI had turned on a series of small lights that dotted its torso and arms, bright enough to illuminate the cell. The rest of them went dark, conserving power. After a while, Geena curled up and went to sleep.

"Poor kid," said Olaf. "She's still learning to be a citizen, and it hasn't been easy."

"Why did you bring her?" Lydia asked.

"She's twice as strong as I am, and her reflexes make me look slow; and now that she is officially a person, the galaxy belongs to her as much as to the rest of us."

Time passed. Lydia used the suit's waste disposal system, then drank some water. It was ice-cold and refreshing, with a faint citrus flavor. At last, the cell door opened. Bin entered. The door closed behind him. His helmeted head turned, taking in all of them and pausing briefly to regard Mantis, who looked like an odd floor lamp.

"What an experience!" Bin said.

"Tell us," Olaf responded.

"They have no men, none at all. The entire colony is female and parthenogenic. Our species has always responded to stress by producing clone-daughters, but never exclusively. How could we, since it's men who do the nurturing?"

There was a scratching noise above them. Mantis shone a light on the ceiling grill. A bright blue eye stared down at them. "Mere vermin," Mantis said. "We can ignore it."

"The women here use milk from animals, which they modify till it is almost like a father's milk," Bin continued. "And they build artificial pouches as warm as real ones. These machines even produce the sounds a pouchling ought to hear: the beat of her father's heart, the whisper of his breathing, the tender words he speaks to her. It works, they tell me. They are able to raise children, though it seems to me these Atch women are harsher than the women on my home planet, having never known a father's care." The little man paced around. "Do you have any idea how uncomfortable it is to keep one's tail inside a suit, even one that flows like this one? I wanted to tear this thing off and twitch, quiver, coil, thrash! But I didn't."

"That was wise," said Mantis.

"They remember the Age of Religious War," Bin said. "They know that an STL fleet left the system, taking everyone who believed in the new religion: the goddess who was paired with a god, thereby providing the universe with nurture as well as creation. The people in the fleet were my ancestors. They settled the planet that humans call Lifeline.

"The people who stayed here thought they would have peace, now that the rebels were gone. But the people who believed in the new religion were—it turned out—the least typical members of their two sexes. The women were unusually gentle and reasonable. The men were unusually bold and firm.

"The people remaining were at far ends of the sexual continua from those who left. The women were fiercely violent, the men so timid and mild that they could do nothing to restrain the women." Bin stopped pacing and turned to face the rest of them, though they couldn't see his face, only the dark eye band in his silver helmet. "There may have been other causes for the wars that began. According to Marx and Engels, in their magnificent Manifesto, the process of industrialization — and the accumulation of the capital necessary for industrialization — is always unsettling. All the bases of traditional social life are undermined and brought down. 'All that is solid melts into air, all that is holy is profaned, and people are at last compelled to face with sober senses their real conditions of life.'

"Obviously, the culture here was industrialized. How else could it build an STL fleet? Maybe this process had already destabilized society and led to the new religion. According to Marx and Engels, this could not happen. Industrial societies destroy religions, rather than create them. But we are not human. Our history may have taken another course. Be that as it may, the people here were left with an old religion, damaged by decades of religious war, with women who were too violent and men who were too meek, and with an economic system characterized by — as Marx and Engels say — 'constant revolutionizing of production, uninterrupted disturbance of all social conditions, everlasting uncertainty and agitation.'

"The violence on the home world escalated; and constant warfare produced the stress that led to parthenogenesis, or so the scientists in this colony believe. By this time the Atch men had descended to a condition close to slavery. The women, producing eggs without fertilization and too busy with violence to court and marry in the traditional way, forced the men to nurture their clone-daughters.

"Remember what Atch men are like. When we mate — or if we are exposed to a woman who is reproducing — we go through extensive hormonal and physical changes. Our genitals become a brooding pouch. Into this pouch go our wife's or lover's eggs, which we hatch and feed with father's milk and raise to adulthood. The process of transformation is almost always irreversible. Most men become fathers only once, though their single clutch may contain as many as ten children.

"Because all sense of community had broken down, the Atch women did not consider the results of forcing men to raise their clones. Of course these children were female. The creation of male children requires male genetic material. If men were not allowed to reproduce, there could be no pouches and no father's milk for future generations."

Bin paused, breathless and obviously upset. Above them, the vermin made more scrabbling noises.

"The women on the planet — producing eggs without fertilization and in unending numbers — struggled for control of brooding men. The men, in turn, tried to resist the entire process. By caring for the clone-children, they were losing their chance to have children of their own. As a group, we are generous; but our generosity is not perfect. We would prefer to brood and nurture our own genetic material. Resistance came too late. The men were too weak. They were imprisoned, becoming animals in stalls, valued only for their pouches."

"This is terrible," said Geena.

"As bad as Earth in the old days, before the AIs arrived and saved us from ourselves," said Lydia.

"Did human women treat human men this way?" Geena asked. "Is there any way to remove my human genes?"

"Human men treated human women badly," said Olaf.

"This badly?" asked Geena in a tone of horror.

"I can't say," Olaf answered. "I'm not a historian."

Bin continued. "It's possible that some women had foresight and tried to maintain the old methods of reproduction. But most focused on immediate survival for themselves and their clones. After decades of war, it no longer seemed possible to plan for a better future.

"Things were not quite as bad in the space colonies, the scientists told me. Unlike the home world, which had over two billion people at various levels of technological advancement, the colonies were small, with uniformly high levels of technology. They had ways to care for children without turning men into animals. Nonetheless, they lost their men. It's possible the scientists were not entirely honest with me. Why did the men disappear, if they were treated fairly?

"In the end, the home world collapsed into savagery. If any Atch continue to exist on the surface, they do so without the benefits of civilization."

"The people here never went down?" Olaf asked.

"That is another story." Bin took a deep breath, then looked at his silver-gloved hands. The fingers had curled into claws. "I am still new to politics," he said. "How does one endure the knowledge of injustice and murder?"

"With difficulty," Lydia said.

After a moment the little man exhaled; his fingers uncurled; and he continued. "There were eight colonies in moonlets, seven orbiting the Atch home and one orbiting the next planet out. One colony succumbed to internal conflict. Another was invaded by refugees from the home world who managed to kill off the colonists, but could not maintain the colony. That moonlet went silent, after pleas for help that were not answered. The other colonies survived. They had STL ships. Hundreds of automatic satellites, many of them still in operation, surrounded the home planet; and there were more throughout the home system. The remaining colonies were self-sufficient and had the resources of the system: every planet, moon, planetoid, and comet. It did not seem so bad a situation.

"For a generation or two, they remained on guard in case more refugees came up from the home planet. But then the home world Atch lost the ability to build rockets. The colonists maintained radio communication with Atsatch, but their relatives could not reach them; and they had no desire to descend into the chaos on the surface.

"Once the men on the home world were gone, the problem of caring for children became severe. The radio messages described attempts to brood eggs under electric lights or in heaps of warm sand. Once hatched, if they did hatch, the pouchlings were kept in bags carried by their mothers or other women. Since no normal woman lactates, the pouchlings were fed milk from animals and specially-made liquid food. Most died.

"The population of the home planet dropped to a fraction of what it had been. The wars continued. Now the women sought female slaves to care for their children while they fought. The slaves laid eggs, of course. They were allowed to keep one or two, but most were destroyed so that they could devote themselves to their owner's eggs.

"The Atch on the surface were no longer able to maintain a culture with modern technology. They were too few and too obsessed with war and reproduction. One by one, the radios went silent. Signs of intelligent life — rail lines, ocean fleets, cultivated fields, roads, and cities — disappeared. This did not happen quickly. The colonists watched a very slow death."

"And never went down?" Olaf asked again.

"I said, there is another story. There is something in this system that's hostile to Atch. It was not here when my ancestors first began to explore. Nor was it here when the STL fleet left. But sometime during the wars of reproduction, accidents began to happen — not on the home world, but in the planetary system. The thing, whatever it may be, does not attack the home world directly or the Atch who live in colonies, unless they try to travel or communicate. But the automated satellites have all gone silent, and any ship that tries to leave its home dock is destroyed. If a moonlet sends a message to another moonlet — they no longer do this — a piece of space debris will strike the sender. It may or may not destroy the colony; but it is always a discouraging experience."

"This is disturbing information," Mantis said.

"Are you in communication with the courier?" Olaf asked.

"I have tried, but no. The moonlet is shielded against radiation, always a danger to life forms in space, and I am getting interference from its internal power and communication systems."

Olaf drew a gun. "Time to go."

"I agree," Bin said. "The women here make me uneasy."

Above them the vermin shrieked.

"That really is an irritating sound." Olaf lifted his gun.

"Don't shoot," said Bin. "The vermin is talking to us. I heard a word distinctly. It's Old High Atch for 'help.'" The little man glanced up and spoke rapidly in Atch. The vermin screamed a reply.

"I asked if it wanted our help or was offering to help us. 'Both,' it said."

"Tell it to move up the air duct," Olaf said.

Bin spoke. The vermin shrieked and scrabbled. Olaf fiddled with his gun's controls, then deftly cut the grill free. It slammed down onto their cell floor with a clang, and Olaf kicked it to one side. Several seconds later, a body fell from the duct. Landing, it tumbled over, then sat up on its hind legs. It was larger than the animals Lydia had seen previously: almost a meter tall in sitting position. Its eyes shone iridescent blue in Mantis's light. Its dark back alternated scales and bristly hair. The tail, as bare as a rat's tail, was pale blue and ended in a tuft of hair, from which emerged sharp, black spines. Hardly pleasant to look at, she thought. But the Goxhat were not pleasant to look at either, and not everyone liked the appearance of Divers. The animal shrieked some more. What a voice!

"It says it will lead us to people who can help us. They live farther in toward the axis of the moon."

"No," said Olaf. "We need to get back to the courier, and to the stargate." He turned to the cell door and cut it open, ignoring the animal, which continued to make pleading or arguing noises. Olaf holstered his gun and kicked the door. A section fell into the hall. Olaf leaned out, looked around, then stepped through the hole. "Okay, gang, let's move."

They followed, the animal coming last.

"Tell that creature, if he or she wants to be helpful, he or she can lead us to the dock. If there's something in this system that destroys ships and stations, our courier and gate need to know."

Bin spoke to the animal, who replied. "His name is Tail Striker, and he will guide us to the dock. Though he will continue pleading with us en route, and I have promised to translate."

"It's a deal," said Olaf.

"Have we set off alarms, do you think?" Lydia asked.

"Almost certainly," Olaf said.

Bin spoke to the animal, and it bounded down the corridor. They followed, Mantis first, lit up like an Exile Tree. Except for the light emitted by the AI and the suits, the way was dark. Animals lurked at the edge of visibility, smaller than Striker, but apparently the same species. Now and then, Lydia saw a blue eye flash or the flick of a spine-tipped tail. They reached an intersection. Striker turned into a another corridor, shrieking.

"The Atch live close to the surface, where the G is highest," Bin said. "These creatures — they call themselves hladcha — have their homes close to the axis. The Atch know this region poorly, from old maps. We will go along the axis to the dock."

The corridor was straight. The G dropped rapidly. Soon they were using handholds, moving from one to the next like their arboreal ancestors. To tell the truth, Lydia didn't know if Bin's ancestors were arboreal — the way he moved suggested they were not — and Mantis had no ancestors. Still, the AI was graceful. For a while, Striker did the same as the rest of them, leaping and scrambling from hold to hold. Once the G was low enough so the rest of them were floating more than walking or swinging, he stopped. Clinging to a handhold, he gathered himself and jumped across the corridor. His body turned in midair, so that he landed hind feet first. Barely pausing, he jumped again, powerful hind legs propelling him back across. In this fashion, bouncing from side to side in a zigzag pattern, he moved rapidly out of sight.

"He is good," said Olaf.

They followed as quickly as they could and found Striker clutching a handhold, waiting. He made a noise.

"He says we're slow," Bin said.

They continued, Striker bouncing and the rest of them moving hand over hand, till Geena tried to imitate the hladcha. She was too big and too clumsy in her suit. Instead of turning in midair and landing neatly, she hit the wall head first and tumbled away, limbs going in all directions. Olaf caught her. "Goddamit, Geena. This is no time for experimentation. Are you all right?"

"I think so."

"You could have broken your neck."

"Not while wearing one of our suits," Mantis said. "If you had given it a warning, Geena, it would have prevented the tumble. Please remember that these suits are your allies. Work with them!"

A scream came out of the dark ahead of them. It was Striker, calling them on.

The journey was like a nightmare. Lydia had to move as quickly as possible in an environment where she was slow and clumsy. Darkness surrounded her; she had no idea where she was; enemies were on her trail; she did not trust her guide; and the suit she wore made her uneasy. She had never worn intelligent clothing before.

You will get used to it, her AI said. *You have gotten used to me.*

A not entirely reassuring thought.

At length a dim glow appeared in the distance. The light at the end of the tunnel, Lydia thought. Striker, ahead of them as always, shrieked.

"Stop here," Bin translated over the intercom.

They reached the hladcha and paused. Just beyond him, the tunnel ended, and they looked out into a large spherical room. There was no balcony or guard rail, simply the unprotected rim of the tunnel. Lydia grabbed a handhold, afraid of falling, though that made little sense here. She leaned forward, looking down.

A thick metal rod ran through the room's middle, exiting through tunnels on either side. A sleek metal car rested atop the rod; another car was fastened underneath. The car below the rod was lit inside. That was their source of illumination. Other tunnel openings dotted the curving walls. Lines went between them. After a moment, she realized these were ladders or tracks, small in the distance and unoccupied.

Bridges crossed the room. Some of these were simply round beams, like the bars of a jungle gym, with hoops and large clips hanging below them. Others had tracks on top. One, which led from the wall to the lower railway car, was a tube of metal mesh large enough for a person to walk — or float — through.

There ought to be machines on the tracks, Lydia thought, and the hoops ought to be moving. Surely they were a kind of conveyor belt. At least there was light, and the railcars looked as if they might be functional.

Striker squealed, then launched himself into air. A moment later, his small body hit a round beam. He twirled around it, came upright and dove to another farther down, making another spectacular, spinning landing, then another dive.

"I think we're supposed to follow," Olaf said. Striker landed on top of the mesh tube, scrambled along it and wriggled through the narrow space between catwalk and car.

"How?" asked Bin.

"Jump," said Mantis.

"I can't do that," Bin said. "I don't like flying."

"Let your suit do it for you," Mantis said.

As the AI spoke, Lydia's suit took two steps forward to the tunnel's edge.

"Hey!" she said.

Not to worry, the suit told her and leaped. It and she went down in a slow fall that turned into a tumble. Shit, thought Lydia. Her arms went out without her volition, and one hand caught a loop. She swung, straightening herself out and losing momentum. After a moment or two, the hand let go. Her fall continued: a slow drift now, like a dry leaf in still autumn air.

Olaf went past her, shouting, "Crazy Horse!" She glanced down and saw him hit the mesh tube feet first, so hard she expected him to bounce off. But his shoes took hold. He staggered, straightened, and laughed.

Geena came after him and landed on all fours. She pushed herself quickly upright.

Lydia kept drifting, barely moving.

Olaf will have us in his reach shortly, her suit told her. *Wings will not be necessary.*

Wings? she thought.

Olaf reached up and grabbed her feet, pulling her to the tube's surface. Her boots touched down with an audible click. They had become magnetic, Lydia realized.

For the time being, her suit said.

Why didn't you do that before? Lydia asked.

It wasn't necessary before.

Olaf crouched and opened a hatch. They climbed into the tube. "Where is Mantis?" Lydia asked. "And Bin?"

"They are coming via the ladders," Olaf said. "Bin must really object to flying."

"I found it interesting," Geena said. "Like climbing in trees or on cliffs, but with more freedom. I hope to be able to do it again."

Striker came down the tube from the railcar, shrieking. On a bet, he was saying, "come on" or "hurry up."

"I think we'll wait," said Olaf.

They stayed in the tube, Striker bouncing around impatiently, till Mantis and Bin arrived.

Striker made another noise and led them into the railcar, the lower one, which was brightly lit. Entering, they found no seats. But there were handholds on the walls, and a row of poles went down the car's center. An Atch floated next to one of these, using one hand to keep herself in position. She was female, of course, tall and very thin. Though it was always difficult to judge such things in other species, Lydia thought she was old. Like the council of scientists, she wore a costume that looked like cutoff overalls. The costume was frayed at the edges, badly faded and patched in several places. Her feet, which hung just above the car floor, were bare and curled into claws.

Olaf drew a gun. The woman spoke.

"'You need not threaten me. I am a friend,'" Mantis translated. "'Using the axial railway, I will take you to your ship. As we ride, Striker and I will explain the situation here. I am the true Hereditary Xenobiologist. I was replaced, because I told my colleagues that the animals we raise for meat and milk are intelligent. Afraid for my life, I fled here to live among vermin. I notice that your shoes are adhering to the floor. Nonetheless, you might want to take hold of a pole. It will help you balance. We're about to start.'"

The car door closed, and the car began to move, sliding out of the spherical room into a pitch-black tunnel. Lydia felt acceleration tug at her. Across from her, Striker grabbed a pole with all four paws.

The woman spoke again, Mantis translating. "'Striker's ancestors were laboratory animals, smaller than he is, native to our home world. We brought them up here and tinkered with their genes, adding material from various animals, including the Atch. Some of this was done out of curiosity, some in an attempt to cure Atch diseases, especially the diseases common in low gravity. This is why Striker and his kind live so well in zero G.

"'When civilization collapsed on our home world, we turned the hladcha from test animals into food animals and especially into milk-producing animals, since our men were vanishing.'"

"Vanishing," muttered Bin in humanish. "Being destroyed!"

That led to a question, which Lydia asked. "Could you have used your technology to save the men? And recreate the old method of reproduction?"

Mantis translated. After a moment, the woman replied. "'Possibly we could have. For all I know, some work was done, back when we were more skilled than we are now. If so, it did not produce the results we needed. Maybe the researchers were forced to stop. I know there were ethical qualms about experimenting with people and questions about the need for men. Scholars — ethical thinkers — argued that our dignity as rational beings is diminished by having a male sex. Men may belong to an earlier, more primitive stage in our development, which we have transcended.'"

A noise came through the radio. Lydia decided it was Bin snapping his teeth together.

The woman stopped speaking for a moment, then continued, with Mantis translating.

"'I'm not a historian. I don't know what happened to the Atch men. But I do know what happened to the research done on the hladcha. The animals developed intelligence and the ability to speak, though my former colleagues refuse to believe this, in spite of my excellent proof! I don't believe the hladcha are as intelligent as we are. They certainly don't speak as well, and we do need to milk them if our children are going to survive; but it seems wrong to turn them into meat.'"

Striker shrieked, and Bin took up the translation. "'There are different kinds of hladcha. Some of us have been turned into factories for milk. Others are factories of meat. Living in dark pits like animals, learning nothing, our kin are not able to be anything except animals. We, whose ancestors escaped, can think and speak. A cause for joy! But not enough! As long as we are here in this moon, we are not safe. We want to escape.'"

"Where?" asked Olaf.

"'Anywhere!'"

The car continued to glide through darkness. The Atch woman spoke again.

"'We have reached a moral impasse,'" Mantis translated. "'And we're not doing well practically. Apparently, sexual reproduction serves a purpose, or else living in space is the problem. We are less hardy than our ancestors. Genetic defects are accumulating. Worst of all, because we are clones, our traits do not change except through mutation; and as is well known, most mutations are not beneficial.

"'The Venomous Bug line always dies young. The Gliding Hoppers have trouble laying eggs. My own line lacks imagination, though we used to have it. I do not think we are going to survive, unless we take action.'"

"What do you think has to change?" asked Olaf.

The woman answered. Mantis translated, "'We must leave this moonlet, and it's possible, though I don't like the idea, that we need to recreate men.'" She looked at Bin. "'If you were still fertile, such a recreation would not be difficult. But now — we have lost so much technology! I doubt that we can make men from your cells, though we certainly ought to try. If my former colleagues had any imagination, they would have tried to culture you at once.'"

"Why do you dislike the idea of recreating men?" Bin asked, first in Old High Atchin, then in humanish.

"'Look at you,'" the woman answered. "'Little, soft, and cringing! An insult to our species! Yet in your genitalia, if you still had them, could be the salvation of my world.'"

The car slid to a stop. They were in another spherical room, this one much smaller.

"'This is the dock station,'" the Atch woman said, with Bin translating. "'It's at the base of our old docking pylon. In the old days, we had elevators to take us from this level to the pylon's top. But these no longer work. You will have to leave as you entered, through one of the pylon's maintenance tunnels. Once you are out of the station, turn left and look for a hatch that says "maintenance access." It leads to the same tunnel you used when you entered our world. It will take you back to your space craft.'"

"How do you know so much?" Lydia asked.

"'The wild hladcha spy everywhere,'" the woman said. "'Watch out for soldiers! The council knows that you entered our colony here. They may be willing to let you leave, but I doubt it. They are all cowards! As bad as men! They'll be afraid of angering the enemy that lurks in space. It will be safer — in their opinion — to keep you as prisoners or kill you and dissect you. They can't let you wander free. Your existence calls into question a long-established way of life. Men and aliens! Who knows what they may mean or do? If nothing else, you are the end of life as we have known it for many long hands of years.'"

"Make sure your suits are closed," said Mantis.

Lydia checked her fastenings. Everything was shut.

The Atch woman spoke again, and Mantis translated, "'I am too old to go with you and too valuable. I alone have studied wild hladcha. But Striker is young and hardy. Take him! He will be his people's ambassador.'"

"It will be dangerous," Olaf said, and Mantis repeated the message.

Striker shrieked.

"He is willing to go," said Mantis.

The car door opened. They clanked out through another mesh tube. At the end was another door, which opened as they approached it. Mantis said, "I will go first, followed by Lydia and Precious Bin."

"Why?" asked Olaf.

"They have AIs interwoven with their nervous systems and connected to their suits. If there is trouble, I do not want to rely on the slow reflexes of living beings."

After a moment, Olaf nodded. He had a gun out. So did Geena. Striker was upside down, clinging to the ceiling of the tube, his spiny tail flicking nervously. Mantis said something to the hladcha, then led the way out. Lydia followed, her mouth dry, and found herself in a brightly lit tunnel. Twenty meters in front of her were black figures: Atch in atmosphere suits. They floated, tethered to handholds in the walls. This left their hands free, and the hands held rifles. Whatever the guns fired, it must not produce a recoil. Well, thought Lydia, light could kill.

A commanding voice spoke from above them.

"'Surrender or die,'" muttered Bin.

Remain calm, said Lydia's suit. *We are taking over.*

Mantis stepped to the side.

Knife-sharp spines emerged all over Bin's suit. The spines whirled around their long axes, flashing brilliantly. Electricity arced from tip to tip, and something — the suit or the whirling spines — made noise: a painful, high, metallic scream combined with a deep thrum that vibrated inside Lydia's teeth and bones. Her suit was becoming spiny as well, she realized, and her spines were also whirling and generating sparks.

Bin moved toward the soldiers, his arms raised, covered with turning spines. Flashing and sparking and filling the entire tunnel, the little Atch male advanced. Lydia followed.

"Jesus H. Christ," said Olaf's voice inside her suit.

A couple of Atch lifted their rifles into position. Lydia saw a flash of light. She must have been looking directly at the laser as it fired. But her eyes seemed fine, as did the rest of her. Had the light hit her?

Yes, her suit said. *I told you I was good.*

Bin's suit continued to advance, whirling and sparking. A soldier threw her rifle into the air, yanked her tether free and fled hand over hand. Another followed. Then all the soldiers were fleeing, scrambling and kicking and bouncing off walls and one another.

Bin paused. After a moment or two, Lydia noticed electricity no longer sparked and arced around him. Then she noticed that Bin's spines were no longer whirling. Instead, they were melting, shortening, losing their edges and points. The same was happening to her suit, Lydia was certain, though she couldn't see the process clearly. She had the start of a truly huge headache.

Obviously, we could have used force, her suit said. *But psychology seemed like a better idea. Given the sound range of Atch speech, we expected the noise we generated to be disturbing.*

The noise stopped. O blessed silence!

And we expected the sight of whirling knives and electric sparks to disturb, especially when these came at them in the shape of people. All intelligent life forms have stories about monsters; and the worst monsters look like them with subtle differences—in this case, sparks and knives.

Are you guys getting more sophisticated? Lydia asked.

About intelligent life? Possibly. But there is still much to learn. That's why you are here.

Bin's suit had reassumed its original shape. So had hers. Mantis came to join them.

"I am less well armored than your suits," the AI said. "And I lack many of their resources. For that reason, I stepped aside. I hope this will not give you a bad impression of me. I know that humans value physical courage, even when it makes no sense — as is usually the case with the heroes of your holoplays, who could certainly find other ways to solve their problems."

Lydia couldn't think of a reply. She was shaking in her atmosphere suit; the headache felt like an ax going through the middle of her head; and she kept seeing the thing Bin had become — a man made of knives — over and over, like a flashback in a holodrama.

"We should keep moving," Olaf said, arriving next to her.

A short distance farther on, they came to a door.

"'Airlock and maintenance access,'" Bin read. "'Before entering, be sure you have the proper equipment, and that the equipment is working.'"

"What about Striker?" Lydia asked.

Geena unfastened the front of her suit. "Tell him to climb in. It won't be for long."

"Are you crazy?" asked Olaf.

"I trust him; and if he harms me, he will be trapped in this suit with whatever he has done."

Bin spoke to Striker. The hladcha leaped onto Geena and was fastened into her suit. They entered the airlock and cycled through. Beyond it was a tunnel and a ladder. They began to climb.

Up and up. At length a voice spoke on the intercom, "You are returning. Good. I was beginning to worry."

The courier?

Yes, said her AI.

"Keep climbing straight up," the courier said. "You are directly beneath me."

It was another nightmarish journey through darkness, dogged by fear, fatigue, and aching feet. Even with the suit's help and the lack of gravity, Lydia had trouble climbing. At least she didn't have to worry about falling. The suit would catch her, and if it didn't, she would simply float.

They came to another airlock, the same one through which they had entered the moonlet. She recognized the damage. Climbing out, her headlight shone on the silver bars of the courier's docking cradle. Buddha! She heaved a sigh of relief. The courier's outer door was open. Light poured out. Safe at last. She climbed the last few meters into the courier's airlock.

The door closed behind them and locked. Air whispered in. They took off their suits and put them in lockers. For a moment or two or three, they floated in the airlock, motionless except for Striker, who was drifting back and forth across the room above them like a swimmer doing slow laps. Buddha she was tired, Lydia thought.

"I have some news," the courier said.

"Yes?" asked Olaf.

"It isn't good."

"Tell us," said Olaf in an impatient tone.

"The stargate has been destroyed."

Lydia heard the words with disbelief. How could that happen? The AIs kept saying they were invulnerable.

We only said our technology is superior to anything we have yet encountered, her AI put in.

Geena began moaning.

Olaf reached up and patted the pseudo-ape's broad, strong shoulder. "Do you know what happened?" he asked the courier.

"There is another AI in the system. An STL explorer, one of the machines we send out in large numbers to learn about the universe. Barring accident, they can last for hundreds of thousands of years. This particular explorer was here before the stargate arrived, but kept quiet, following an orbit it had established long ago. Most likely it was in sleep mode until something roused it, either the stargate's arrival in the system or my departure for this moonlet. Remember that we did not signal the Atch until I was in motion. Then both I and the stargate broadcast as widely as possible.

"After we arrived here and you had entered the moonlet, the explorer sent a signal to the stargate. They spoke briefly. The explorer said it was a mistake to contact the Atch. There are some things we are not meant to know. One is the existence of an intelligent life form as violent and self-destructive as the species here.

"The explorer established a quarantine. Atch may survive on the home world. It doesn't know or care. They barely survive in space and will be soon gone, unless someone intervenes to save them. The explorer is keeping watch to make sure they do not spread.

"It's very old," the courier continued. "Programs have failed, and files have been lost or damaged. If it ever knew about other self-destructive species — humanity, for example — it is no longer able to access that information. Its idea of intelligent life is the Goxhat."

A species known for their lack of personal identity. The Goxhat language did not distinguish between "I" and "we." For them, murder was the same as suicide. Like suicide, it sometimes happened, but was always evidence of a serious form of mental illness called "fragmentation." War was impossible for them, and institutionalized oppression was unknown, since it required that hundreds or thousands of Goxhat go crazy all at once in a way that caused them to lose their sense of unity while retaining their ability to act together. Utterly impossible, Goxhat psychologists said. Other species might be able to live oxymoronic lives. The Goxhat could not.

It would've been a nasty shock to go from the Goxhat to the people in this system. Was the shock severe enough to explain this AI's behavior? Lydia asked the question.

"No," said the courier. "This is a systems failure. What we have here is a machine that has gone bad. Of course the stargate disagreed with it. They argued, and the explorer blew the gate apart. Fortunately, the gate sent me a copy of their conversation. I got it just before I saw the light that came from the exploding gate."

"What do we do?" asked Olaf.

"The explorer knows I'm here and is willing—it says—to leave me intact, but only if I get out of space. I would prefer to do so quickly. I don't trust this machine. It may change its mind, if you can call what it has a mind. Please enter my cabin and strap yourself in. I'm about to flee to the planet below."

Mantis extended arms and legs till it filled one end of the airlock, its limbs braced against floor, ceiling, and all four walls.

The rest of them went into the courier's cabin, Geena plucking Striker from midair where he was still doing laps. Anxious energy, thought Lydia, or the pacing of an animal in a cage. They were all trapped, now that the stargate was gone.

The hladcha shrieked.

Mantis said something in answer. It seemed to settle Striker. He snuggled against Geena's shirt.

They strapped in. Lydia felt a jolt as the courier released its hold on the dock. The screen above her showed darkness. There were more vibrations. The little steering rockets were firing, edging the courier backward into space.

PART TWO: THE WORLD

Once they were clear of the moonlet, the main rockets fired. Acceleration pressed Lydia into her seat. She found herself gripping the seat's arms and forced her hands to let go. There was always something a little disturbing about going up or down the gravity well of an Earth-sized planet, even though she had done it many times, most often by elevator or skyhook. The first mode of transport was her favorite. Who could complain about a smooth glide up or down in a car firmly attached to a cable? A skyhook wasn't bad. Taking a rocket plane to or from the skyhook's terminus didn't seem much worse than ordinary flying. But this — dropping like a stone through the full extent of a planet's atmosphere — always struck her as a little scary; and this time there was a rogue AI somewhere above them, which might decide to blow them into fiery fragments at any moment.

Maybe you should think of something else, her AI said. *My organic components are affected by the hormones you secrete when afraid.*

Think of it as a learning experience, Lydia answered.

There are some things AIs are not meant to know.

After a while the courier spoke, raising its voice above the sound of its rockets. "I'm not going in entirely blind. The stargate made a preliminary survey of the planet and sent the data to me before it was destroyed. I will double-check the data as we descend.

"Unless I find information that makes me change my mind, our goal is a large continent in the northern hemisphere. It appears to be made of two plates that have run together, pushing the planetary crust up into a series of mountain ranges. These divide the continent, going approximately north to south. The highest peaks exceed eight thousand meters. The region to the east lies in a rain shadow. This is our destination."

"Why?" asked Lydia.

"Two reasons. The rogue is orbiting the planet south of the equator. If we land far enough north, we will have the planet between us and it.

"Secondly, an arid region is not likely to support a large population. After your reception in the moonlet, I do not want to meet a lot of Atch. If they are here — if they survive on the surface of the planet — I want to be able to see them coming."

There was silence after that, except for the noises the courier made as it decelerated and leveled out. The screen above Lydia showed a dark blue sky, empty of stars. Clouds appeared. The courier dropped farther, and the screen went gray.

"There are low mountains along the continent's eastern coast, at present hidden by rain clouds," the courier said. "Beyond these is a plain and then an arid basin. At the basin's center is a lake, surrounded by salt flats. I will land there."

The clouds vanished, and the screen showed a hazy, blue-green sky. The sound of the courier's engines changed. Coming in, thought Lydia. If the courier was like a human rocket plane, wings would be unfolding, wheels dropping and locking.

Now she heard a new noise, coming through the roar of the engines. It was a disturbing, high-pitched whine. Not the sound of wings or wheels. Lydia looked around. Geena sat next to her. The pseudo-ape's shaggy red head was pressed back into her seat's cushions, and her eyes were tightly closed. She held the hladcha in her arms. The little alien's mouth was open. He was crying. That was the whine.

The courier hit ground, rolled, braked with a scream and slowed. Lydia exhaled. "It's okay," she told the hladcha and Geena and herself. "We're down."

The pseudo-ape opened dark eyes. Her big hands began to stroke the hladcha. His keening grew softer. "I have just counted," Geena said. "I flew four times on my home planet. Three were airplane flights, and one was a rocket plane that took us — Olaf and me — to the bottom of the Tchel skyhook. Then there was a space flight to the Tchel stargate. Then there was the flight to the Atch moonlet. Then this. Seven flights so far in my life. Do they become easier?"

"Yes," said Lydia. "Especially if you aren't escaping a crazed AI."

"I will try to avoid that situation," Geena said. "Calm, Striker, calm. We're safe. We're on the ground."

The courier rolled to a stop. The screen above Lydia show a white plain rimmed with yellow mountains. The sky above the mountains was dusty blue-green.

The courier said, "We are in the arid basin. There's a lake at the basin's center, almost certainly saline. As I descended, I saw a grid pattern in the ground next to the lake. There are mounds in the grid that may have been buildings once."

"Radiation?" asked Olaf.

"Normal for a planet with this atmosphere, orbiting a star like this one. The temperature is 27 degrees Celsius. The humidity is negligible. The air is breathable, though you still may want to wear atmosphere suits if you leave me to explore."

"Time for a conference." Olaf unlocked his seat and swung it around, so he was facing Geena and Lydia. After a moment, Bin did the same.

"Mantis?" said Olaf. "Can you hear us?"

"Yes."

"Courier, did the gate get a message out of the system before it was destroyed?"

"Yes, through its stargate."

"So your colleagues — comrades — whatever — know what happened."

"Yes."

"Then all we have to do is stay alive till the AIs come to rescue us. Where's the nearest other gate?"

"Five light years from here," the courier said.

Olaf grinned, or was it a grimace? "Then, if the AIs make our rescue a priority and send one of their fast STL ships, it will be here in 20 years. Am I right?"

"It could be sooner," the courier replied cautiously. "Twelve years is possible."

The AIs had STL ships that traveled half the speed of light. This was news to Lydia.

"There's water," Olaf continued. "If it proves undrinkable, we can distill it. The atmosphere is breathable. Bin and Striker should be able to metabolize the local proteins. The rest of us cannot; and we need to worry about vitamin deficiencies and toxic quantities of minerals." He looked up, since the courier's voice came from the ceiling. "What kind of supplies do you have?"

"Emergency rations for thirty days. After that, we will have to rely on my ability to synthesize necessary organic compounds or alter the local compounds, so that you can metabolize them."

"You have a chemistry lab?" Lydia asked,

"Yes," said the courier.

"We know your needs," Mantis added. "And we are, as I said before, rationally prudent."

Olaf grinned or grimaced a second time. "So, we have air, water, food, weapons, and a new world to explore. Twelve years should pass quickly!"

"Are you being ironic?" Lydia asked.

"Actually, I'm being pissed. I thought this was going to be a quick job. In, out, and home with enough money to build a new set of tourist cabins."

"I thought the same," said Geena.

"Instead, I'm going to spend twelve years in a desert, eating God knows what, but I doubt it will be manna."

Striker made a noise. "He wants to know what we've been talking about," Bin said, then spoke to the hladcha in Old High Atchin.

Striker listened intently, while Geena stroked his scaly back. His ears were large and edged with fur. They flickered now and then in response to what he heard. Finally, he spoke. Bin translated. "I told him we're exploring here, but not that we are trapped. He's willing to join us in exploration, though he says he feels oddly heavy. Maybe, if we travel, we will find a place with less G, he says."

The courier produced images, taken on the way down. They showed the salt flats, white and almost featureless, a green lake and two rivers. Both rivers and the lake were edged with bright yellow vegetation.

"We'll go to the nearest river," Olaf said. "Take a look around. If there are no problems, we'll follow the river to the lake. I want to look at those ruins. Lydia, I know you have a state-of-the-art recorder. Use it. We may be trapped like rats, but we are also the first humans to discover an alien lost civilization."

"I'm not human," said Bin. "And this civilization is not alien to me."

"Well, you're the first something."

"The first Atch to come back to our ancestral home."

"That's worth recording."

Olaf was taking charge, Lydia realized. Well, he was a professional guide, with years of wilderness experience, and she had no better ideas for how to handle the current situation.

"What about Striker?" asked Bin.

"I'll carry him," said Geena.

"You've taken a liking to him," Olaf said.

"We are alike. Both of us were made by science for dubious reasons. Now we must remake ourselves."

Night came, filling the overhead screens with stars. A brilliant point of light moved among the stars: a moonlet, maybe the one from which they'd escaped. Lydia went to sleep uncomfortably in her seat. She woke several times and shifted position. Nothing helped much. She hated self-pity, but at the moment—looking at a decade on this world—she felt almost sorry for herself. Still, it could be worse. She had companions.

Two humans, if you count Geena as human, her AI said. *An Atch, a hladcha, eight AIs and a lot of very sophisticated equipment. Have faith, Lydia!*

She slept again, woke, and saw dawn on the screen above her, poking its orange fingers above a shadowy mountain range. Buddha, she was stiff! She rose and stretched, then used the sanitary facilities. On impulse, she opened the airlock door. Mantis was in the airlock.

The AI had returned to its normal size and shape and stood in a corner. "I'm going out," said Lydia.

"You might consider putting on your suit," the AI said.

Lydia considered and put the suit on, feeling a brief twinge as it connected with her AI. It was much less painful than the first time. She opened the lock's outer door. A stair unfolded in front of her. When it stopped moving, Lydia descended. The gravity felt right, which meant it was close to the G of her home world and most other human planets. Above her, sunlight filled the sky. A few clouds floated like gauze banners. The ground, still in shadow, stretched into the distance, empty of life. She listened and heard nothing, except the sound Mantis made, coming down the courier's stairs.

The AI stopped at the foot of the stairs and extended sensors.

"You keep watch. Yell, if anything dangerous appears." She took a deep breath, settled her mind and began to do Tai Chi — not the classic version, invented on Sol Three, but Master Ho's version, designed for humanity's new life among the stars. How does one achieve harmony with earth and heaven, if there are many earths and heaven is a black void? The same way one gets to Carnegie Hall, according to Master Ho. Lydia practiced, feeling a little awkward in the atmosphere suit, while the planet's primary rose above the eastern mountains. She ended when it was completely visible, shining through gauzy clouds, dimmer than any human sun she knew and improbably golden.

Behind her, Olaf said, "I didn't know you did Tai Chi."

She turned. He was standing at the bottom of the stairs, also in his atmosphere suit, which glittered with reflected sunlight.

"I studied when I was in prison," Lydia said. "I don't do much these days, but it seemed like the right response to this."

The white salt plain. The hazy blue-green sky.

Olaf looked around. "This is beautiful in its way, I guess. I prefer my home Let's go in to breakfast. It's going to be a busy day."

By late morning, they were all outside. Olaf said, "This helmet isn't going to work. I want my peripheral vision and my hearing and sense of smell."

"The suit can keep watch for you," said Mantis.

"I prefer to do my own watching," Olaf said and unfastened his helmet It settled onto his shoulders like a thick collar or a scarf. "I don't see that disease is a problem — or bug bites, given what the courier has said about differences in biochemistry. If I can't eat the local life, then most likely it can't eat me. And you said the suits can close quickly. But I'm going to need a hat."

"The suit will tell you where that tool is kept," Mantis said.

After a moment, Olaf felt along the suit's belt, pulling out a narrow silver rod. He shook the rod; it opened into a hat with a wide, stiff brim. The shape reminded Lydia of the hat Odysseus wore in ancient human art. Olaf pulled off his helmet and put on the hat. Dark glasses dropped over his eyes. A cord snugged itself under his chin.

"Holy shit. An automatic hat." He laughed.

A moment later Bin raised a hand to his helmet.

"You share this world's biology," Mantis warned him. "You may well be at risk."

"I will take the chance," Bin said. "I want to see and smell and feel this world."

"We brought you here to learn from you," Mantis replied after a moment. "I will not second-guess your decisions. If you get anything, the courier can probably cure it."

Bin's helmet folded onto his shoulders, and he found his hat, fumbling it open. Lydia and Geena followed his example.

They made an odd group, Lydia thought: silver-hatted, in bulbous silver suits. Geena carried Striker on her shoulder, the hladcha clutching the folds of her helmet. Her hat shaded him, except for his tail, which hung down in sunlight, twitching occasionally.

They started toward the river, Olaf leading. The plain was hard and flat, easy walking. Lydia's suit was light and cool and — at the moment — silent. Her companions, looking around at the new planet, were also silent. She heard only the scuff and crunch of footsteps. After a while, she looked back. The courier was following them, rolling over the flat plain, spinning up a small cloud of dust.

Why? Lydia asked her AI.

Why not? It is intelligent and designed for exploration. Why should it sit in one place and wait for information? Why do you think it landed here, in a place where it can maneuver?

The primary moved to noon position. The air brushing her face was hot. Lydia sipped water from her suit's tube. Ahead of them a yellow band expanded: the vegetation along the river. Here and there, plants appeared on the plain, hand-sized and roughly hand-shaped, six thick stalks radiating from a fleshy base. Although the vegetation ahead of them was yellow, these plants were green.

"I know them," said Bin suddenly. "They're in old stories. According to the stories, they grow where Atch are buried. I don't think so. No one would bury an Atch, even an enemy, here."

She recorded the plants, then turned to record the salt plain, dazzling in sunlight, and the courier rolling slowly after them.

The hand plants grew more common, and new plants appeared between them. These had round, thick, shiny yellow leaves. Finally, they pushed through spiny bushes. There was animal life now: long, thin fliers with transparent wings. Their eyes, two in number, were huge. Lydia recorded them. Predators, she thought, though not of anything large. They were ten centimeters at most.

"The courier is stopping," Mantis announced. "It's afraid of harming the native life forms if it rolls over them. It will keep in touch with us by radio, and if we decide to travel along the river, it will follow on the plain."

Ahead of them were trees with yellow foliage and bulbous trunks.

"Jug trees," said Bin. "I know them from old stories also. This really is my home world."

The vegetation beneath the trees was low and soft, the color of an orange, with a sharp aroma. She'd smelled that tang more than a kay away, the moment she undid her helmet. Overhead, on branches, animals cried. They looked like a cross between birds and lizards.

They reached the river finally. Clear water flowed over tawny sand. On the far side, maybe ten meters away, a large quadruped rested on a sandbar: another predator with a mouth full of ragged teeth. The broad, flat body looked designed for swimming rather than running. Lydia recorded it and the lizard-birds. One glided down through sunlight, flashing iridescent green. Her recorder got it, along with a toothy yawn from the sandbar predator.

"No dipping in the water," Olaf said. "And we should be alert for animals on the ground." He gestured at something at his feet. "This, my children, is a path."

Craning, she made it out: a band of bare dirt that paralleled the river.

They took the path, walking single file, Olaf first, then Mantis. The guide had a gun out; the AI's head bristled with extended sensors.

As often happened when one was ready for danger, none appeared. They walked for three hours along the path, in the shadow of the jug trees. Now and then, in deep places in the river, they saw long animals like fish undulating. In one place, a quadruped swam with a fish held firmly between ragged teeth. By mid-afternoon, they reached the lake or rather its marshy edge, full of flying bugs and lizard-birds. Beyond the marsh was a glittering expanse of water.

"We want to go west," said Mantis. "The courier is waiting for us there, next to a ruin."

They turned away from the river, keeping the marsh on their right. The salt plain had ended in sand dunes, which they climbed over. At the bottom of one hollow was a badly worn pot, made of something that looked like plastic. Bin picked it up. "An artifact."

"Not new," said Olaf. "And not attractive."

"Still." Bin's silver hands caressed the plastic. "It's something my ancestors made." He carried it till they came to a brick wall, half covered by sand. The bricks had a pattern stamped in them over and over. "Writing." Bin crouched. "It says, 'Repository of Very Great Value.' I think it's a temple or a bank."

Bin rose, leaving the pot next to the wall—almost as an offering, Lydia thought.

They continued, moving between low mounds with yellow plants growing on them. Here and there, the wind —or something else—had swept sand away, revealing stone pavement. At last they saw the courier, stopped next to an especially tall mound. The remains, Lydia realized, of a step pyramid. She could make out walls and terraces. The walls were glazed brick, chipped and pitted. Lydia saw figures in relief: Atch men in a procession, some holding children, others with bulging pouches.

"This is certainly a temple," said Bin. "Or a child care center."

Steps led up. They climbed, Olaf still first, gun in hand. Every terrace had decorated walls: always men and children. As they climbed, Lydia looked around, seeing other mounds, the courier, the lake. A wind blew off the water, moist and salty.

On top of the pyramid was a block of stone, cubical and plain. A desiccated body lay on top.

"Atch," said Bin after several moments. "A woman. Murdered." He tapped the region of blackness around the body. "This is dried blood, and this." He touched the gaping throat—oh, so lightly. "Is the fatal wound."

"She was sacrificed," Lydia said.

"Yes," said the little Atch. "Though none of the old stories mention sacrifice. War, yes! Terrible violence! But nothing like this. My ancestors were civilized."

"You aren't remembering the stories you were told in the moonlet," Olaf pointed out. "The men in stalls, treated like animals."

"That is true," said Bin. "I don't know what to do. Every Atch deserves burial. Yet—"

"We'll leave her," said Olaf. "I'm surprised the birds haven't been at her."

Bin took another look. "I think her body has been coated with something."

Lydia made a recording, then they went back down to the courier and shed their suits. Striker moved around their feet, crying softly.

"'Heavy! Heavy!'" said Bin in translation. "'Is there no end to heaviness?'"

They slept in the cabin. In the morning, Lydia went out and practiced Tai Chi. Rising over the eastern mountains, the primary shed golden light.

They ate breakfast in the courier. After they were done, Mantis said, "I set out perimeter alarms last night. They have reported no disturbance, except a few nocturnal animals, which the alarms frightened away. We can stay here safely for another day or two."

"Okay," said Olaf.

They pitched tents next to the courier. Like the suits, these were silver, but not—thank the Buddha—intelligent. When that was done, they hiked back to the river. "We need water," said Olaf. "Firewood and bugs."

"Bugs?" asked Bin.

"For the courier to analyze, so it can synthesis food for us."

"The courier will make bugs?" asked Geena in an anxious tone. "I don't want to eat bugs. Doc Schmidt, who created my people through genetic manipulation, told us humans were top predators. Lesser beings, far down on the food chain, eat things like bugs."

"Viruses are the top predators," said Olaf. "Doc Schmidt was a lunatic, and the bugs are for analysis, not eating."

"Let me gather the bugs," said Mantis. "My sensory equipment is more sophisticated than yours, making finer discriminations over a far wider spectrum. In addition, I can process data more quickly and react long before you are able to."

"Okay," Olaf replied.

The AI reached down and opened boxes on its legs, invisible till now. "Pockets," it said. "Like the ones on Olaf and Geena's trousers." It plucked a huge-eyed predator from the air, putting it in a box, then scooped something with many segments off the ground. The second creature went in a second box. Mantis wandered off among the trees.

"We will gather fallen branches," said Olaf. "It's more our speed."

They carried the wood back to camp. Mantis gave its bugs to the courier. Olaf wandered around looking at the ground, then finally returned with a small black cube. "Is this an alarm?" he asked.

"Yes," said Mantis. "Put it down."

Olaf bent and set the cube — which was perfect black, the black of space — on the ground. It lifted itself up on four tiny, angular legs and walked away from the courier, back toward the place where Olaf had found it.

"It didn't go off," said Olaf.

"It knows you are not a threat," Mantis said.

"Is it intelligent?"

"Yes, but it has narrow interests."

Night fell. Geena built a fire. After some discussion, they all took off their suits. A zillion stars blazed in the desert sky. Lydia glanced around at her comrades. Olaf and Geena were dressed in hunters' tan, Bin in an embroidered tunic. She wore tights and a blousy shirt. Striker wore only his fur and scales, Mantis only his metal.

Olaf said, "I talked to the courier. The water here has trace contaminants: minerals and organic molecules, also microbes, which can be filtered out. We may be able to drink it directly out of the rivers. We can certainly drink it if distilled. We'll get a report on the local biochemistry in a couple of days."

Striker, curled up next to Geena, lifted his head and made a low, sad sound.

"'How long will we be here?'" Bin asked for the hladcha.

Olaf rubbed his face and hair. "Tell him ten years."

Bin warbled. The hladcha shrieked and warbled in reply.

"He says he'll be dead before then. The life span of his species is not long. He will die alone, among aliens."

Geena picked up the hladcha and held him, whispering words of comfort in a language he could not understand.

After a while, Lydia went to bed. In her absence, her atmosphere suit had morphed into a sleeping bag. She crawled in and was asleep at once.

Dawn woke her. Next to her Geena snored softly, one arm around Striker, who was snoring, too, a sound like a purr. Lydia crawled out of the tent. An atmosphere suit stood at the edge of camp. She went over. "Olaf?"

"I am Precious Bin's suit," it replied. "He didn't want to sleep in me, so I am standing guard and observing the planet. We are programmed to be protective and curious, so long as curiosity does not interfere with protection."

"Do you like the planet?"

"I was manufactured for this expedition. I have no previous experience to act as a standard or comparison. The atmosphere is neither crushing nor corrosive — except for the oxygen it contains, which does corrode, but also keeps you and your companions alive. The temperature is moderate. Visibility is good. I can perceive no immediate danger. If I had no life forms to protect, I would explore."

Her comrades woke and made breakfast. Bin shared his food with Striker, though the hladcha ate little. "He says the food tastes strange," Bin told them. "Maybe the problem is freeze-drying."

Afterward, Olaf and Lydia put on their suits and walked to the lake. Tall yellow reeds blocked access to the water. The reeds were full of lizard-birds, gliding and crying. Now, in brilliant daylight, Lydia could see the animals' teeth and the claws on their wings. Their feathers flashed metallic blue and green. She recorded.

Olaf said, "I'd stay here, except for the body. I don't know how old it is. Not very, I'm afraid."

"Why do you think they killed her?"

"How can I possibly know? We'll stay here till the courier has finished its analysis, then look for another place to stay." He paused, then added in a quiet, even tone, "I'm finding this situation difficult, even scary. I suppose that means I'm no hero."

"Did you think you were one?"

He laughed. "I saw a lot of Stellar Harvest holos when I was a kid."

"You wanted to grow up to be Ali Khan."

He laughed again.

"It's not a bad ambition," Lydia said. "He's a splendid athlete — even now, at his age — and the gentlest, kindest human you can imagine. But not a hero. An actor."

"Well, then, I'll emulate him and try to act like a hero, though I'm not happy with this situation. Twelve years on an alien planet! And all I know is how to keep tourists from getting eaten by megafauna on my home world."

They walked along the shore till they came to a break in the reeds. Clear water lapped the sand at their feet. A narrow channel led away, edged by three-meter tall reeds. "Interesting," said Olaf, then walked into the channel. He stopped when he was chest deep, pulled his helmet on and fastened it, then ducked under water. Lydia recorded him, wondering what the heck he was doing. He surfaced finally, a bright blue weed draped over his silver shoulders like a lei.

"The channel is artificial," he said when he reached shore. "The reeds along its edges have been cut, mostly below the surface; and someone lost this." He held out his hands. One palm held a knife hilt made of bone and decorated with crisscrossing lines. On the other palm was a stone blade. Obsidian, Lydia suspected. In any case, something black and shiny with a sharp, flaked edge. "Surprising that she left it," Olaf went on. "Maybe she couldn't find it in the sand. I felt it when I stepped on it." He tucked the pieces in his suit belt.

They walked back to the ruined city, keeping close to the shore.

Olaf said, "If the knife is any evidence, we are looking at what we would call a Neolithic technology. Reassuring. I would hate to meet people with a high technology, who were sacrificing members of their species."

They climbed among the ruins. Lydia recorded sandy slopes half covered with vegetation. Olaf, who had a sharper eye than she did, picked up something and handed it to her. Part of a broken pot. It was ceramic, glazed sky-green, with a pattern of white lizard-birds soaring, their clawed wings spread. "Left over from the age of banks and child care centers, I imagine."

She carried it back to camp. They showed both objects to their companions.

"We have come to this," said Bin, holding the broken knife.

"Not you," said Geena. "The people on this planet, who turned intelligent beings into things. May all life forms who use their fellows in a similar way come to a similar end!"

That evening, the courier gave a preliminary report. "Striker can metabolize the organisms here. Precious Bin may have some problems, but will probably survive. Olaf, Lydia, and Geena will starve to death, unless they are poisoned first. I am working on ways to process the local food so it can nourish all of you."

They ate dinner, aware of how little prefab food was left. Mantis set out the alarms, then moved beyond the alarm perimeter into darkness. Why? To guard the camp? Or watch nocturnal animals? Or was it interested it the planet's night sky, brilliant with stars?

Bin's suit looked at him. The little man said, "I will use you tonight. It's cold here after dark." The suit nodded, an oddly human motion, and went to Bin's tent. The rest of them sat by the fire. Finally, one by one, they went to bed.

Lydia woke to the sound of the courier, speaking in a firm tone. "Please wake up! There is a possibility of danger!" Her sleeping bag morphed into a suit around her, and she scrambled out of the tent, gun in hand.

The courier had turned on external spotlights, illuminating half a dozen Atch. The aliens sat on quadrupeds. They were all holding long, dangerous looking spears. Four of the spears had shining black blades. Stone, thought Lydia. The other two were tipped with long narrow pieces of something white. Plastic, she was almost certain. Bin warbled. The Atch looked surprised. Lydia recorded the animals: angular, scaly, and dark blue, with shimmery manes on their shoulders and chests. The Atch on top wore trousers, but no shirts. Their broad chests were flat and covered with intricate patterns in shades of green. White bone bracelets shone on their muscular, green arms. They looked uneasy, and the quadrupeds were clearly restless. But the riders and their steeds stood their ground.

Bin spoke again. An Atch answered, and he translated. "'I speak your language, though imperfectly. Our bards use it to chant ancient lays. Hru! Hru! The deeds of strong women! Hru! Hru! Action and death!'"

There was more hooting and warbling. Bin said, "I have told them we are travelers from a far distant place. We mean no harm. We are merely passing through."

The Atch woman answered. "'What about the slaves?'" Bin said in translation. "'Have you seen them?'"

"What slaves?" asked Olaf, and Bin repeated the question in Old High Atch.

The Atch woman answered, hooting and warbling. Striker cowered against Geena.

"'The women who should care for our children,'" Bin translated. "'Many have escaped. They live in the wilderness and come here to offer sacrifices, asking the Goddess to bring back men, so women can be free. We intend to capture them and return them to their proper condition.'" Bin added, "I don't know what to say."

"Ask them what kind of sacrifices the slaves make," Olaf suggested.

There was another exchange; Bin translated the reply. "'They offer the lives of their former owners, if they are able to capture us. Otherwise, they offer one of their own people, usually a just-hatched child. They have no good source of milk in the marshes. Most of their offspring die before the time for weaning. Therefore, they steal the children of our slaves and our own children when they are young, before we cut off their tails, turning them into true women. They make them — our children and the children of our slaves — into enemies!'"

"Tell them there's the body of an adult woman on top of the child care pyramid," Olaf said.

Bin did. One of the women — not the speaker — warbled and dismounted.

Two other women joined her on the ground. Together, they began to climb the pyramid. Their trousers had no openings in back. They really did not have tails. It seemed abnormal. An Arch should have something to flick and curl.

The speaker hooted at Bin, and he spoke in humanish. "The woman who dismounted first said, 'It must be my sister, who is named Cunning Hladcha. She has been missing for more than twenty days.'"

The remaining woman stayed where they were, astride their animals. In the dark beyond them, something gleamed: Mantis, standing outside the light.

"Ask them where they get milk," Olaf said. He had spotted Mantis as well, Lydia thought, and was trying to distract the Atch women.

Bin asked. The translator replied. "'Our animals,'" Bin said. "'We ride the stallions and geldings. The mares feed their young and ours.'"

No one spoke for a while. The animals flicked long ears and stamped broad, two-toed feet. Their riders watched Lydia and her comrades. Amazing the riders hadn't fled, since all of them — even Bin — were in atmosphere suits, the helmets up and closed. What a sight they must be, to people who knew nothing about space!

Finally, the women who had climbed the steps came down. Two carried the body, wrapped in a blanket. The third woman walked behind. Her arms had been cut and streamed orange blood. The body was set down on pavement. The bleeding woman spoke.

Lydia's suit translated. *It is her sister, murdered by slaves. There must be revenge for this.*

The other women hooted and whistled. *They agree,* the suit added.

When did you learn Old High Atchin? Lydia asked.

Yesterday. I downloaded from Mantis. My knowledge is not perfect. The language here is not identical to the one in Mantis's files; and some of the information did not transfer in a form that makes sense to me. Either Mantis and I are not entirely compatible, though we are supposed to be; or I am encountering a logic problem. The languages made up by living beings are notoriously illogical.

In front of her, an Atch rider pulled out a black stone knife and used it to cut her arms, while hooting. '*I will hunt down the mud-eaters, the women with tails,*' Lydia's suit translated. '*They will oooo, the milkless ones! My sharp spear will go entirely through the stealers of children! My knife will cut the ooo who hide in reeds!*' *Problems remain, but you can get the gist.*

You bet, thought Lydia.

The other women clicked and whistled, shaking their spears. Lydia felt queasy. Maybe all lost civilizations were like this. She had hoped for something more utopian.

The women loaded their dead relative on an animal, tying her in place. Then the spokeswomen warbled.

"'You must come with us,'" Bin said. "'This is a holy place, forbidden to slaves and monsters.'"

"Tell them we'll leave," Olaf said. "But we'll go in our own direction. I don't trust these people worth a damn."

"You want me to translate the last sentence?" Bin asked.

"No."

Bin warbled. The women bared sharp teeth. Their spokeswoman spoke again.

"'Why should we trust you to do as your promise? You are monsters.'"

In answer, Bin undid his helmet and pulled it off, revealing his Atch head.

The riders whistled. The spokeswoman said, "'We thought you were light-reflected-off-water monsters.'"

What?

Bin continued his translation. "'They existed in the time of our ancestors and served our ancestors, as our slaves serve us.'"

Machines, thought Lydia, glancing at her companions. How would people without metal describe the way metal shone? It flashed silver like sunlight off water on a bright day. It gleamed gray like water under a cloudy sky.

"'In the time of our ancestors, the monsters were servile. Now, if they still exist, they are timid. I was surprised that you stood your ground. But now I see that you're our kin, come down from the night sky. We know the people there are still alive. Their swift boats glide among the stars. Why are you here? What harm do you intend?'"

One of the riders — she couldn't tell which one — whistled. As one, they threw their spears. What coordination! Bin's suit reacted before he could. The helmet flashed up around his head and closed. A spear bounced off his eye band. Another hit his chest, dropping to the ground. Lydia felt a blow to her shoulder. *A bruise at most*, her suit told her. Two more spears bounced off Olaf and Geena.

Olaf drew his gun, aiming it at the wood piled up for tomorrow's fire. A moment later, the wood burst into flames. "Tell them I can set them all on fire."

Bin spoke. A woman whistled. The riders turned their animals and vanished into the night.

"Apparently, they're still angry at the people in the space colonies," Olaf said. "Amazing how long intelligent beings can hold a grudge."

"Not AIs," said Mantis, coming into the light.

"What about your comrade, who has decided to quarantine this system?" Olaf asked.

"That isn't a grudge. It's a serious malfunction."

"Whatever you want to call it. Why didn't the alarms go off?"

"They warned me and the courier," Mantis said. "I asked the alarms to do nothing more. A loud noise would have frightened the Atch. I thought we should speak to them, if possible. We are here to make contact."

Olaf frowned, then nodded. "We had better sleep in the courier."

They did. Folded into her seat, Lydia slept badly, waking often. The cabin air was stuffy. She heard small noises: Olaf's even breathing. Geena's erratic snore. Striker whimpering in his sleep. Like Lydia, he must be having bad dreams.

They broke camp in the morning, loading everything into the courier. Olaf and Geena went to look at the trail left by the riders. When they returned, Olaf said, "They went east. Therefore, we'll go west along the lake shore."

They walked, wearing their suits and silver hats. The courier rolled after them. Ten years in this place, fighting off people who owned slaves and sacrificed one another. The prospect was discouraging, though the day was lovely. High clouds dimmed the golden sun; a cool wind blew off the lake. Around noon they came to a beach of white sand. Waves rolled gently in. White birds glided over the water.

"They're stronger fliers than the birds in the forest," Olaf said. "Maybe they have to be."

Lydia and Bin walked at the water's edge. There was a line of debris: shells, small pieces of wood, thin strands of weed. The lake must be new and no more salty than an ocean. It clearly contained life. One of the white birds splashed down, then rose with something in its claws.

She wanted to be out of her suit, feeling the wind through her clothing, walking barefoot through the water.

Too dangerous, said her AI. The suit agreed.

Do you think the machines here were intelligent? Lydia asked.

The light-reflecting monsters? her AI replied. *Almost certainly not. We have never found true artificial intelligence outside ourselves. Human machines can mimic thinking, but nothing is going on below the surface except rapid counting, which is NOT the same as thought. Only our long-vanished creators made machines that are self-aware.*

Just as well, Lydia thought, imagining intelligent machines—creatures like her AI—watching the culture that made them collapse into savagery.

We do not have the biochemical bases for emotions. Therefore, we do not feel grief.

Does nothing happen when you see this? Or the ruins of the cities of your makers? asked Lydia.

There is something, her suit said. *We call it ****. It means a recognition that something—an event or experiment—cannot be repeated, and we have not learned what we wanted to learn from it.*

How would you translate it? she asked.

There was a silence, while — Lydia assumed — the suit went rapidly through vocabulary files.

In Old High Atchin, it would be 'oooo.' In human-ish, the best equivalent is 'pissed off.' A sense of some-thing wasted.

Bin picked up a shell, a delicate spiral, and held it out to her. "We have these on my world."

"There are things that repeat from planet to planet," Lydia said.

"Cruelty," Bin said sadly. "Violence." He bent, gently replacing the shell.

Efficient shapes, said her AI. *Physics and engineering.*

The beach ended. They walked past reeds bending in the wind. Toward evening, they came to another beach. They set up their tents on the warm sand. Olaf and Geena gathered driftwood. It must come down the rivers, Lydia thought, float in the lake for awhile and finally wash up here, as white as bone or salt.

Before they lit the fire, Mantis planted the alarms — a good, long distance out this time. The sun went down. Stars appeared, so bright the lake reflected them. Lydia looked at her companions, their bare faces lit by the fire. Olaf was growing a beard, she noticed. The stubble gleamed redly. Auburn must be his hair's true color.

"I'm trying to decide if the mountains might be saf-er," he said.

"No," said Mantis. "We need a flat place for the cou-rier."

"Maybe we should look for another plain, something more desolate than this."

"You need food," said the courier. "I can transform organic material, but I can't make it out of nothing."

"You need water," Mantis added. "We can condense it out of the atmosphere, if necessary. But it would make more sense to find liquid water and filter or distill it. The organic material the courier needs is more likely to be found near water."

"Another plain with water," said Olaf.

"I will look at the recordings I took as we came down," said the courier.

They went to bed. The night was quiet. Lydia woke at dawn and went out to practice Tai Chi. She left her suit behind this time. It really was uncomfortable to practice in, and she ought to be safe if she stayed within the alarm perimeter.

Yes, said her AI.

Striker was at the water's edge, sniffing the debris. His long, bare, spine-tipped tail dragged in the sand. Poor fellow! He had bounced around so energetically in zero G.

He came over to her and shrieked. Her suit was back in the tent, but AI translated. *Everything smells edible. But the tastes are wrong.*

You know Old High Atchin too?

I downloaded from the suit.

Buddha, she would love to learn languages this easily.

I would not describe the process of learning the language of any life form as easy, though I do better than other AIs, since I have access to your biochemistry. Imagine learning a language when half of everything is missing. What does humanish mean, without the ebb and flow of neurotransmitters and hormones, muscles tightening and relaxing, acid burning in the stomach, sweat glands producing sweat, mucus membranes growing wet or dry?

Could we change the subject? Lydia asked, bent down, and picked up Striker. He looked so unhappy crouching in the sand, visibly crushed by gravity.

Nestled in her arms and surprisingly heavy, he whined. *I want to go home*, said Lydia's AI.

Can you use my voice? she asked without speaking. If you can, tell him that we all want to go home or at least away from this planet.

My control over your muscles is improving, but speech is a complicated process. I will try.

She felt the damnedest sensation in her throat, first tension, then a tremor. Her tongue flicked in her mouth — up, down, back, and to the front. Her lips opened; strange noises came out. Striker started. A moment later, he relaxed. His large ears unfolded. She thought she saw comprehension in his bright blue eyes.

Cold comfort, of course, to say they shared his feelings. If they were lucky, they would live to see rescue and travel into space. Striker would not. Maybe they would die as well, leaving the courier, Mantis, the suits, and her AI to tell their story.

"Bury us," she said out loud. "I don't want to dry up in the sun, like the woman on top of the pyramid."

Yes.

Striker struggled. She put him down, and he went back to the water's edge, turning over pieces of debris with his paws, licking them with a long, pale blue tongue.

After breakfast, the courier announced, "I have found another landing place. Like this one it's flat and arid. There are canyons along its southern edge. Vegetation grows in the canyons; and my recordings show several gleams that are almost certainly light on the surface of rivers. After consulting my planetology files, I have concluded that the plain is the bed of a large lake, made at the end of a glacial period, most likely by an ice dam. When the dam melted, the water poured out through the canyons, and some still remains."

"I vote yes," said Olaf.

One by one, the rest agreed. Lydia voted last. She had, she realized, a strong desire to meet the escaped slaves. Her early life had been devoted to liberation, and she still had an interest in seeing how freedom might work. The Atch women had not made it sound appealing. Still, they spoke as bosses, and bosses always accused working people of beastly behavior. Only supervision made workers human, according to the ruling class.

And you said Precious Bin had out-of-date politics, her AI remarked.

I told him Marx might not apply to his species, Lydia answered.

They loaded their camp into the courier and climbed on board, settling themselves in the cabin and fastening their safety webs.

"Ready?" asked the courier.

They answered, "Yes." Engines roared to life. The courier rolled briefly and lifted. As it did so, the screen above her came on, showing bare, white ground, then a band of yellow vegetation. The marshes along the lake, she thought. They kept rising; and the screen filled with water, pocked with waves and troughs, shining like hammered silver.

The sound of the engines changed. The courier was rising steeply now, tilting to one side. The lake was gone.

Instead she saw mountains, haze-grayed, wrinkling into the distance.

"This will be a slower trip than the one coming in," the courier said to them. "I'm not sure where the rogue AI is. It may have moved to a new position and be able to watch us. If so, I don't want to give the impression that we're trying to leave the planet. It was very clear in its instructions. It wants no space travel by the Atch or us.

"We will be in the air for four human standard hours. Make yourselves comfortable."

Hard to be comfortable, while thinking of a crazed AI somewhere above them. What if it changed its mind and decide to destroy them, even though they had obeyed instructions?

There is no point in worrying about that, If it happens, it happens.

Thank you for that input, she told her AI.

You are welcome.

Watching the screen, she decided they were traveling west and south. The courier's shadow — with broad wings now — moved over bare slopes and valleys. They were still rising, but so were the mountains. Patches of snow appeared here and there. After a while, she saw more vegetation, dotting the mountain sides and growing densely in the valley bottoms.

"As I told you, a series of mountain ranges go down the middle of this continent. They create the dry plain on which we landed. We are crossing the easternmost of these ranges," the courier announced.

After a while, the mountains diminished in size. Now, they flew over low hills. The land remained arid.

"There are more mountains to the west," the courier said. "They limit rainfall, though this region is not as dry as the plain we just left."

They began to descend. The screen showed a flat plain, marked here and there by dry river beds. If there was any vegetation, she couldn't see it. The courier dropped farther and slowed until it was hovering in midair. Then it dropped again, going straight down till it touched ground. It bounced gently. The engines quieted. A far different planetary landing that their first one!

The first time we were coming in as quickly as was safe, her AI said. *From a great height, with a lot of velocity.*

Looking at her screen, Lydia saw the sky: overcast, low, and gray. Clearly there was more moisture here than at their first landing site.

"I saw no evidence of intelligent life coming in," the courier said. "You can disembark safely."

Their suits were in the airlock. They put them on and climbed out. The ground was dull brown, dusty, and dotted with small orange plants. Some were like pin cushions, round and spiny. Others were fleshy stalks, as if something — the planet, maybe — was giving them the finger over and over.

"We'll spend the night here," said Olaf. "Everyone sleep in his or her suit. I'll set out the perimeter alarms, and Mantis — if it's willing — can stand guard."

"Of course," the AI said.

They'd brought driftwood from the salt lake — how many kays away? Geena built a fire. They ate and slept. In the morning, they started south, hiking over the plain. The courier followed, rolling.

At midday the clouds broke apart, letting sunlight through. An improvement, though not a huge one. There were bugs flying around the orange plants. Lydia saw no flowers to pollinate; most likely the bugs were eating the plants or one another. Birds sailed overhead, dots in the dusty blue-green sky.

"Carrion eaters, I bet," said Olaf.

On the ground were more bugs, some round and shiny, others long and segmented. Once, Lydia saw a small quadruped that reminded her of the lizards on her home planet. Long, narrow, and gray, the creature had a fin on its back. The lizards on her planet used their fins to regulate temperature. This fellow probably did the same, though the colors—bright blue with yellow edging—suggested it also served to attract mates. "See how strong and healthy and gaudy I am! Surely you want my genetic material for your progeny!" Or maybe the colors conveyed another message. "Watch out! I'm poisonous!"

She made a recording before the little fellow flicked away.

At day's end, they made camp by a dry gully. "This leads to the canyons," the courier said.

The night was quiet, the sky full of unfamiliar stars. How often had she sat on planetary surfaces, looked at the sky and seen nothing familiar? For a brief moment she wished for her native constellations: the Mechanic and the Wrench, the Rocket Ship, the Dancers. Not that she wanted to have them always in the sky. But she wouldn't mind a visit home. It wasn't possible, until the government changed, which did not seem likely to happen anytime soon. It would be better to dream of a visit to Stellar Harvest's home planet, where the constellations were named after famous holoplay characters. If all went well she'd make it back there.

Mantis spent time with the courier, then rejoined the rest of them. "We will reach the plain's rim — the edge of the canyons — tomorrow. They seem worth a look, since they contain water and vegetation. But the courier does not want to try landing in them. If we go down, we will have to go without it."

In the morning, they followed the gully as it descended. Late in the afternoon they came to a rim. The ground dropped abruptly. A broad expanse of eroded land stretched into the distance: deep canyons, buttes, and pinnacles of stone. The highest elevations were in sunlight, their horizontal strata gray, pink, yellow, and white. It was hard to see into the shadowy canyons. But there was vegetation down there, and that almost certainly meant water. They settled and watched light fade from the multicolored landscape. The courier had stopped a short distance away. Glancing back, Lydia could see it, its white body shining in the almost horizontal light. Hard to leave it behind, she thought.

I will protect you, said her suit

She woke later than usual, Geena shaking her shoulder. "Look," the pseudo-ape whispered. Lydia raised her head. Mantis stood at the edge of camp, motionless in the gray dawn light. Striker, looking oddly pale, crouched at the AI's feet. He was sniffing Mantis. Why? And how had he gotten past the alarms?

Something cried out behind her. It was a shrill, joyful noise. A moment later, Striker ran past her, toward— himself? As he passed the camp perimeter, the alarms went off. Buddha, they were loud! Startled, the hladcha stumbled, going over into a somersault. The other Striker whipped around — tail lifted, its end spines clearly visible — and ran toward the canyon rim. For a moment, at the edge, the pale Striker hesitated. Then he jumped and vanished.

The alarms stopped, leaving silence. "That's better," Olaf said. "I imagine he ran out, crying 'landsman, landsman,' to use the language of my ancestors, and triggered the alarms and terrified his relative. Amazing that Striker could move so quickly in planetary G. Joy does strange things."

Striker went to the cliff edge, moving slowly now. Mantis followed. The AI said, "There's a trail leading into the canyon."

They straggled over. Sure enough, a trail wound back and forth over steep, pink slopes. Vegetation dotted the descent: yellow bushes and low, orange patches. The pale hladcha was gone from sight — into a crevice or under a bush, Lydia imagined. Olaf slid a little way down, then crouched on the trail. "Prints. Some small animals with paws. Not hladcha. And something with two toes, about the size of a goat, judging from its stride. It might be a herbivore. Then again, it might not. No evidence of Atch." He stood. "This is our way into the canyon."

Striker spoke. Mantis said, "He grieves that his relative fled. I will talk with the perimeter alarms. Striker should not have set them off. Maybe they became confused, when they saw two hladcha. As I told you, their intelligent is limited."

They breakfasted, broke camp, and started down. As usual, Olaf went first, a gun in his silver hand. Their descent took all day, zigzagging over strata that changed from pink to tan to gray to yellow. The soft stone held fossils made visible by erosion. They climbed past an ancient sea full of shells and found land-dwelling quadrupeds below it. A horned skull stared out of a crumbling cliff wall. The trail wound among massive leg bones.

"Ah, God," said Olaf. "A paleontologist would kill to be here."

"Why?" asked Mantis. "The galaxy is full of life."

"But not intelligent life," Olaf replied. "And even if the Atch were not here, this is an entire evolutionary line taking its own direction. Oh, brave new world! With or without people."

They reached the canyon floor just before dusk. A shallow river ran over stones and among trees. They camped on its bank. There were plenty of fallen branches for the fire.

Supper consisted of rations and water from the suits. When they were done, Mantis set the perimeter alarms, and they took their suits off. What a relief! Lydia ran fingers through her hair, then stretched and breathed deeply. The air was full of alien aromas. The suits, not needed at present, went to the river bank and watched water flow. The rest of them, even Mantis, gathered around the fire. Ruddy light danced over rough, gray tree trunks and the faces of her companions — all tired, except for the AI.

"This may do," Olaf said.

Geena nodded. "I like valleys."

Of course she did, having spent her entire life around Tchel's spectacular rift valley.

"I'm used to flat land and open water," Bin said. "This makes me feel closed-in. But if we're safe here, I'll get used to it."

Olaf rubbed the stubble on his face. "The only problem is the courier. Maybe we can find a place where it can land. Or we could live on top of the canyon and descend to get food and water." He paused, then added, "Ah, God, ten years in this place!"

"Twelve, at least," said Mantis.

"I have been corrected," Olaf said with grim courtesy.

The suits came back from the river. One of them, she couldn't tell which one, said, "We are all interested in the motion of liquid H_2O over an uneven surface in the presence of significant gravity. The complexity is — I don't know the word in humanish — intriguing? Elegant?"

"Either will do," said Olaf.

"But Lydia's suit says it can perceive something besides elegance, and Bin's suit agrees. They have been in direct contact with the AIs implanted in Lydia and Bin's brains. Apparently they have learned something from those AIs, who must have learned it from Lydia and Bin."

How did one explain to a machine what moving water — its sight and sound — did to creatures who came from water and were mostly water still? Not knowing, Lydia kept silent.

The suit continued. "We don't know as yet if what they've learned is useful. Further study is required." It morphed into a sleeping bag. The other suits followed.

"There are times when this situation strikes me as damn odd," Olaf said. "In addition, I don't know which of these bags is mine."

Mantis pointed.

"Thank you."

Mantis identified the other bags. Everyone crawled in. Lydia's bag snugged — or snuggled — around her. She felt a brief twinge, as the suit and her AI connected. *Welcome*, said the suit. *You must tell me about rivers.*

Not now, thought Lydia and went to sleep.

The morning was overcast and dark in the canyon's bottom. They ate without enthusiasm, rations and recycled water again, then broke camp and began hiking along the river.

"We'll take a look around, gather some samples and head back to the courier," Olaf said, clearly the person in charge. This was okay with Lydia, who was feeling a little depressed, due to the gray day and her dim future. On the other hand, the canyon was a stunner. Striped pink and tan walls rose on either side of the river, mostly sheer, though slopes and side-canyons were visible here and there. The river filled most of the bottom, along with its trees and bushes, which lit the shadows with bright yellow leaves. Some kind of animal — a bug, she guessed — buzzed in the low vegetation. Other animals whistled in the high branches. Lydia recorded, imagining a holo play here: Wazati Tloo against the local savages, or Miss Highkick decking interstellar villains with precise blows from her tall, black boots.

The interstellar villains would be better. Her employers didn't like to turn indigenous peoples into villains. Too much of their audience was made up of indigenous peoples. "Never piss off the masses" might have been one of their mottoes. "It's many people with a little money who pay our bills."

Most Stellar Harvest villains were organized criminals, developers, polluters, imperialists, fascists, destroyers of beauty, or crazed religious fanatics belonging to no existing religious sect.

Consider the many dramas in which Ali Khan took on the White Serpent Society, a collection of interstellar drug-dealers who worshipped Adolf Hitler. There were a few angry messages from people on Earth who liked serpents and a few more from historians pointing out the dramas were not historically accurate. For one thing, the criminals had hologram portraits of Adolf Hitler in their shrines, and the portraits always showed Hitler as black. Hardly surprising, since most modern humans were black. It was the best way to deal with the radiation from many different suns. According to the historians, this was wrong and would have been deeply offensive to Hitler.

The Research Department said the historians were right. The Legal Department said it was impossible to libel long-dead dictators. The Marketing Department said that living fascists were a tiny market segment, disliked by their neighbors. "But if you're really worried, next time make Hitler green." The company didn't. Everyone knew that humans were black or brown. To make a human another color would require an explanation; and the holo's nonstop action would have to be stopped, so the audience could learn something that did not interest them. Why should a Goxhat or Atch or Golden — or the overwhelming majority of humans — care about the complexion of someone dead for centuries? Better to leave Hitler black. All the color said was, "This person is human."

Thinking about those discussions, Lydia began to miss the Stellar Harvest home office. Enough self-pity, she told herself finally. Think of the positive aspects of this situation. A dozen years without the Stellar Harvest accounting department. Her equipment was close to indestructible and would easily store twelve years worth of data. She would record their struggle to survive, maybe even make a work of art. With Olaf here, her sex life needn't end. There was Geena as well. The AIs, while not available as sexual partners, were wonderful protection.

Yes, said her suit.

Also good company, said the AI in her brain.

By noon the sky had cleared. Brilliant sunlight poured into the canyon, which had become narrow and twisty. Trees still grew on the far bank, but their side of the river was bare, except for a scattering of small plants. The trail wound among huge boulders. Like the cliffs from which they'd fallen, the boulders were striped tan and yellow. There were fossils: odd-looking animals like fish with feet. Had they been leaving the ocean, Lydia wondered, or returning to it? Either way, they had died before achieving their destination.

The trail turned a corner around a really huge boulder. In front of them, in the middle of the trail, was a tall Atch in a long, tan and yellow striped robe. She looked relaxed, standing easily, but the thing she leaned on was a spear. The tip shone. Metal, thought Lydia. Brown metal. Bronze.

The woman spoke quickly.

"We are surrounded," Bin said. "Look up."

Lydia did. Archers with drawn bows stood atop the boulders. Like the woman on the ground, they wore long robes, striped in the canyon colors. A hladcha sat next to one of the archers, looking down with interest, large ears unfolded. Its fur was cream-colored, its rows of scales almost white.

The woman spoke again. "'Do not make any sudden motions,'" Bin translated. "'In fact, make no motions at all.'"

All of their helmets were folded down.

We can react more quickly than you or the Atch, her AI said. *Rely on us.*

"Tell her we mean no harm," said Olaf. "We're only passing through."

Bin and the women conversed, then Bin spoke in humanish. "She says, 'You appear to be metal monsters except for your heads. Are they real heads or masks? If they are real, are you wearing them as trophies, or do they belong to you?'"

Olaf said, "Tell her the heads are real and belong to us."

Bin spoke. The woman was silent for a while. Finally, she spoke. This time, Lydia heard the translation from her AI.

'*Are your bodies really metal? How is this possible? And what kind of metal is it? The color is like silver or tin, but I've never seen either shine so brightly or remain fluid after cooling.*'

Olaf said, "What are the suits?"

"A combination of alloys," said Mantis. "I doubt that a more exact description would mean anything to the Atch or you. The important thing is the material's structure, which varies. At times and in places, it's crystalline. At other times and places, it behaves like an amorphous solid, a liquid or even an organic molecule. Imagine something that has the qualities of iron, glass, water, and silk."

"Tell her the suits are iron," said Olaf.

Bin spoke. The woman straightened up, no longer leaning on her spear. She answered sharply. Oh no, thought Lydia. Another fight.

"'You know how to work iron?'" Bin translated. "'Can you teach us? If not, do you have iron to trade?'"

There was more talk. Olaf said they had both knowledge and objects that might be of value to the Atch, who were starting to look like businesswomen, albeit with weapons. Lydia considered recording the negotiations, but decided not to. It was too dangerous. She would have to move, if only a little.

I will make a record, said her AI.

Would the recording get the beauty and the terror of the scene? The glint of the spear tips, the women's avid faces?

I will do the best I can.

Finally the Atch speaker invited everyone to their camp. "'The trail you've been following was used by animals,'" the spear-woman said. "'The trail for people was across the river. We were hoping you wouldn't find it. If you had, you would have seen footprints and realized that people were nearby. Trapping you would have been more difficult.'"

Olaf groaned softly.

Guided by the Atch, they forded. The water was shallow and clear. On the far side, behind a screen of trees, was the Atch camp: yellow tents and large, blue-gray quadrupeds.

"Wixi," said Bin. "I recognize them from the old stories." Their broad heads bore two sets of curving horns.

The spear-woman spoke. Mantis translated. "'We're traders, and this region has bandits. Because of this, we send our hladcha out as scouts. One found you. If you had been ordinary criminals, we would have tried to avoid you. From the sound of Sneaker's report, you were both odd and rich in metal. Therefore, we set a trap. Now that we have you, we can begin to negotiate. Two things—above all—matter to traveling merchants. New information and new goods. We are especially interested in metal, since we live in a degraded era, which has forgotten most of what our ancestors knew about metallurgy.'"

They sat on a patterned rug outside the largest tent. Women brought cups of hot liquid. Bin explained that most of them came from a far distant place, where the food and drink were different. They could drink nothing here.

The woman spoke. Mantis translated. "'The heads you wear suggest as much. I'm especially baffled by the person who is entirely metal. Either she has many eyes or none. But one of you looks Atch, and the hladcha traveling with you looks like a hladcha. Can't the two of you drink our tea? How can we negotiate, if we can't share food and drink?'"

Bin hesitated, then agreed. Striker climbed out of Geena's suit. Cautiously, the two of them sipped the liquid. "Sharp and sour," said Bin after a moment. "I don't like it." Striker squealed. "But he does."

The pale hladcha crept next to the spear-woman. Glancing up, Striker saw it. His fur bristled; and his tail rose over his back in a guard position, the spines that tipped it clearly visible and sharp.

The spear-woman spoke. Bin said, "'This is Sneaker, our best scout and my good friend. Don't fight with him! We should none of us fight with one another, but save our violence for wild animals, bandits, and clan-enemies.'"

Striker's tail went down, followed by his fur, though he still looked wary, glancing often at the other hladcha.

There was more discussion. The traders were going toward a town several days to the west, where the canyons opened onto a plain or large valley. "'You are welcome to travel with us,'" the woman said. "'Though I worry about other merchants. What if they see you in your marvelous metal clothing? Won't they try to step between you and me? Of course they will!'"

"We have a camp on the high plain," Olaf said. "And a comrade waiting for us. Though your invitation is generous, we must return there."

The woman was silent for a while, turning her cup in her hands. Her long, sharp, curving nails clicked against the ceramic. "'What if you betray us?'" she asked finally. "'You might flee to another merchant company or to the distant land you came from.'"

"Tell her we don't intend to return to our land for many years," Olaf said.

The woman listened intently while Bin translated this, then spoke.

"She asks if we are in exile," Bin said. "Has our clan lost some sort of struggle? Though it would surprise her, if we all belonged to the same clan."

Olaf glanced to Lydia. "What am I going to say? I understand business people when they're on vacation or doing business on my home planet. But here — "

"Tell her that we are waiting for comrades to join us," Lydia said to Bin. "Our land is far away, and it will take a long time for them to travel here. But when they come, they will have more metal than she can imagine."

The woman went back to turning her cup. Click, click went her claws. Finally, she said, "'We cannot risk losing you. Nor can we risk letting you fall into the hands of other merchants from other clans. Therefore, we will divide. Half of us will continue on our journey. The rest will go back to your camp with you. I will give my own daughter the task of selling our goods. Though young, she has my abilities. I'll go with you, and to make sure that you don't play some trick on me, I want her to stay with my daughter.'" She pointed at Bin.

This was not the time to mention that Bin wasn't female. It hadn't gotten a good response previously.

"Ask her if her people have slaves?" Lydia said to Bin.

He did. "A few,'" the woman answered. "'They are women who were not able to pay a debt or captured bandits who decided they'd rather serve than be executed. The first become household servants. The second do hard labor.'"

"Where do you get milk for your children?" Lydia asked next.

"'Our beloved wixi,'" the woman said. "'It may not be as good as the father's milk of legend. Who among us will ever know? But most children grow strong on it and gain the traits for which wixi are famous: staunchness, mildness, and loyalty.'"

"Who raises your children?" Lydia asked.

"'Our clan-members. Who else?'"

"Not slaves?"

"'What fool would entrust a child to someone outside the clan? And what kind of clan would make a kinswoman a slave?'"

"What comprises a clan?" Lydia asked finally.

"'Do you know nothing? We are descendants of a single ancestor.'"

Clones, thought Lydia. "Are you all alike?"

"'This is your fifth question, and the last I'm going to answer. Of course we are not all alike. Some are young. Some are old. Our scars are in different places. Our memories are dissimilar. In addition, the lines within our clan have developed differences over time, as happens in every clan, though not — apparently — where you come from. I belong to the First Daughter Line, which is slightly taller than the rest of us and better at trading. Most of our songs come from the Sixth Daughter Line. The Eighth Daughter Line produces the best warriors. The Third Daughter Line puts on weight easily and survives hard times.'"

Bin translated this; they all sat quietly for a while, thinking about inheritance. Were mutations accumulating in the various lines? Lydia wondered. If so, was it harming these folk's chance of survival? How did the savages on the salt plain organize themselves? Were they also at risk for extinction? Did she care about the savages? No, but she felt sympathy for their slaves; and the traders were likable.

Olaf said, "What do you think, Bin? Are you willing to go with the caravan?"

"My suit has assured me that it can defend me."

"It can," Mantis agreed. "And find its way back to the courier, if need be, and communicate with me and the other suits, though only by bouncing a signal off the planet's ionosphere. I prefer straight-line communication, but that requires a working satellite system."

Olaf rubbed his face and hair. The hair's auburn roots were showing. "Ask her what happens after the trip to town."

The woman spoke. Bin said, "'We'd planned to travel farther west, but this is more important. My daughter will join us at your camp, and we'll take you home to our clan-town.'"

"Where is it?" Olaf asked.

"'East of here, where the canyons end, and the high plain tilts down.'"

"Are there any flat areas without trees?"

"'Yes,'" said the spear-woman.

"Well," said Olaf. "What do we do? We can fight our way out of here and hurt some of these people—and maybe get hurt ourselves, or we can go along with this plan. We've landed at two places and found people in both. That suggests to me the planet is inhabited all over, or at least where there's water and a halfway decent climate. If we didn't have these suits, I'd be reluctant to leave any one of us alone. But the suits seem up to anything, and it might be a good idea to have allies if we have to be here a dozen years."

They talked some more, the Atch woman listening intently, though she could not possibly understand a word. Finally Bin agreed to go. "I've never studied the early stages of a mercantile society. Maybe it will give me insight into Marx and Engels."

Lydia made no comment.

They set out midway through the afternoon, taking two wixi loaded with supplies. The caravan leader, whose name was Dream Wix, strode next to the first draft animal, still carrying her spear and using it as a staff. The hladcha Sneaker ran ahead, two archers following him. Their vanguard, thought Lydia. The rear guard was two more archers. A final pair stayed with Lydia, her comrades, and the wixi. Watching all of them, Lydia assumed. At the trail's first turn, she looked back. Bin stood at the edge of the Atch camp, impossible to miss in his shining atmosphere suit. Beside him was the caravan leader's daughter, who looked like a thinner version of her mother. Lydia lifted her hand in farewell, then looked ahead.

The canyon bottom was in shadow, though sunlight still blazed on the wall above them, turning it a glorious rosy pink. The trees in a high side-canyon shone like gold. The narrow sky was bright and absolutely clear. Lydia recorded, imagining her employer's current superstar, Wazati Tloo, in this place. It was the perfect frame for his beauty and grace. Next to her, the second wix plodded, its heavy gait surprisingly rapid. She hurried to keep up.

They made camp at dusk. The Atch set up two yellow tents. Lydia and her companions slept in one, the Atch in the other. Mantis stood guard, along with two archers.

In the morning they climbed out of the canyon. Again, the wixi surprised Lydia, being sure-footed and agile in spite of their bulk. Late in the afternoon their party reached the rim. Lydia was breathing heavily, though the wixi seemed fine, as did the Atch and Olaf and Geena. Clearly she needed more exercise. Maybe she ought to climb a canyon wall every day. The high plain stretched before them. Big, ragged clouds covered most of the sky. A few rays of sunlight slanted between the clouds. Lydia saw the courier, gleaming in the distance.

"'Is that your camp?'" asked Dream Wix through Mantis. "'Is it made of metal?'"

"Yes," said Olaf.

Dark fell as they walked toward the courier. The space ship's external lights came on, blue-white and orange-red.

"Hru!" exclaimed the Atch.

"Are you in communication?" Olaf asked Mantis.

"With the courier? Yes, and with Bin's suit, though its signal is unclear. There must be weather somewhere."

Lightning flashed in the clouds above them.

"No kidding," said Olaf.

The storm broke as they reached the courier, rain pouring from the dark sky. More lightning flashed. By its light, Lydia saw the courier's stairway unfolding. "This is the tallest thing around here," said Olaf. "And it's metal. We need to be inside."

"Yes," said Mantis, then spoke to the Atch leader.

The archers tethered the wixi under one of the courier's wings. Everyone climbed the stairs, entering the courier's airlock.

Light panels shone in the ceiling, walls, and floor. "Greetings," said the courier.

"Hru!" the Atch cried, looking around for the speaker and not finding it.

For a moment, they stood in the airlock, Atch and aliens together in a too small space, all obviously uneasy. Rain poured past the airlock's open door. Wet air blew in. Lightning flashed in the distance.

"Tell the Atch this is our camp. We would like them to put away their weapons," Olaf said. The courier opened one of the airlock's storage cabinets.

Mantis spoke. The Atch consulted in low voices. Finally, Dream Wix spoke, and Mantis translated. "'We intend no harm, but come in peace to exchange goods and information.'"

"We know this," Olaf answered. "But it's out custom to be unarmed in camp."

"'Very well. Remember that we have your companion, and there is more profit and honor in trade than in war.'"

She liked the merchants, Lydia decided.

Dream Wix put her spear in the locker, and the others followed her example. Once the weapons were all inside, the locker door closed. A moment later, the airlock door closed also.

"Hru!" the Atch cried. Dream Wix spoke again, this time sharply.

"She has asked if they are trapped," Mantis said. "I told her no. The door has been closed to keep out the rain."

The Atch did not look reassured, and Sneaker was definitely fluffy now. Hardly surprising. They were, in fact, weaponless and trapped.

"Tell them I will take off my outer covering. They will see that I'm unarmed," Olaf said.

Mantis spoke; Olaf pulled off his suit. Another cabinet opened. He hung the suit inside and stood in front of the Atch: a tall, handsome, black human in the close-fitting clothing most people wore under atmosphere suits. In spite of the suit's internal climate, he had been sweating. Lydia saw stains under his arms and on his back.

"'From top to bottom, you are something entirely new,'" said Dream Wix through Mantis. "'I had not been certain before. I thought your head might be a mask, in spite of what you told me. Are the others as strange as you?'"

"Yes," said Lydia. "But we are going to remain dressed."

Mantis translated. Dream Wix looked unhappy for a moment, then said, "'Maybe this is for the best. I'm not sure I want to see more strangeness.'"

There wasn't room in the cabin for everyone. Mantis asked Dream Wix to enter, while the other Atch stayed in the airlock. The door into the cabin remained open. Every time Lydia glanced around, she saw worried Atch faces.

Dream Wix looked at the cabin, then spoke. "'This is an odd house,'" Mantis said. "'For myself, I prefer cloth when traveling, brick at home. But you clearly understand the secrets of the ancients. I have never seen so much metal. I no longer believe you come from a distant land. A wonder like this could not have been kept secret. Travelers would have brought stories. Metal could have come in trade.

"'In my opinion, you come from the night sky, where our ancestors' kin went in the Final Days. They live up there still, according to legend, and will come down sometime in the future, either to do us good or do us harm.'" Dream Wix turned and stared at them. "'You are not Atch, therefore you are not the people foretold. But I believe you have come from the same place. Is this so?'"

Mantis spoke. Lydia's AI said, *It has told her yes.*

Dream Wix spoke at length. When she paused, Mantis said, "Since we are not the people foretold, she has no opinion about us. She knows we are friendly with one Atch, and that we are wealthy beyond all understanding. Are we willing to trade? She can't see a need for metal tents, but our outerwear looks as if it might be useful, and she would be interested in seeing our knives, swords, hoes, arrowheads, pots, awls, and chisels. In return, she has fine cloth, ornaments of silver and bronze, flavorings from far-distant places, and the finest, whitest, most pure sodium chloride."

"We may not need any of those things," Olaf said. "But we do need allies. Courier, what do you have that can be traded?"

"The contents of my galley," the courier answered.

Olaf nodded. "Geena and I brought some tools and weapons, things that might prove useful if we ended outdoors. I think they can be safely traded. This culture isn't likely to be transformed by folding cups and swisarmi knives."

Lydia had done research on the Americas during her revolutionary days, since they had produced many revolutions, as well as being the last great imperial power. If she remembered correctly, the native cultures of North America had been transformed by comparable trade goods: pots, hoe blades, knives, blankets, brightly colored cloth, and guns. But given their current situation, Lydia wasn't going to argue against trade. If the AIs did rescue them, the AIs would decide what to do about the cultures here.

We always offer intelligent beings the opportunity to travel among the stars. Most members of most species remain on their home planet, except when the planet has become uninhabitable, as was the case with Earth. But some of each species travel. Having made our offer of the stars, we do not intervene further, except when an intelligent species seems on the verge of extinction — as humans were on Earth.

People still live on Earth, Lydia pointed out.

A few. The planet could not possibly support the billions of humans who have spread through space. I am concerned about the hladcha. The ones in the moonlet may well be in danger. I do not know about the hladcha here.

Olaf swung the seats around, so they faced each other. They all sat down, except for Mantis, who tucked itself into a corner. The pale hladcha climbed into Dream Wix's lap. Striker joined Geena. Both looked fluffy, though their tails were down. Geena stroked Striker. Dream Wix did the same to Sneaker.

"Tell her we are willing to trade," Olaf said to Mantis. "But we are going to wait till our friend has been returned to us. Then, we will provide the traders with tools and cookware made from iron and other rare metals. In return, we want friendship and help until others of our kind descend from the night sky."

Mantis spoke, then Dream Wix, then Mantis again.

She has asked how long it will be till the others come down. Mantis has answered that we aren't certain. It might happen soon or in many years. But be assured, Mantis has told her, they will come, bringing trade goods from the stars.

Dream Wix replied. Mantis said, "'According to a local story, the stars are houses or towns. Their light comes from lamps and cooking fires. The story must be true, if the stars produce iron.'"

The stars did produce iron, of course, but not in the way that Dream Wix imagined.

Olaf said, "Ask her if she's willing to help us."

Mantis did, and Dream Wix answered. "She says yes."

"Well, then," Olaf leaned back. "We have a place to stay until we're rescued."

Dream Wix spoke again. "She says she is hungry and tired. She wants to join her kinfolk in the other room. Tomorrow, when the rain has stopped, they will go outside. But tonight, if we are willing, they will stay in our camp. I have told her this is fine."

She rose, still holding Sneaker, and walked into the airlock. The other Atch gathered around her, talking in quiet voices.

"I will watch them," the courier said. "And listen."

Lydia and her comrades ate, then used the sanitary facilities. How long before she could take a real shower, with a flood of hot water and scented liquid soap? Twelve years. In the mean time, she washed her face and hair. Coming back into the cabin, she adjusted her seat to sleep position. The screen above the seat was dark.

She woke to find sunlight streaming through the cabin door. Leaning out of her seat, she saw the airlock's outer door was open and the lock empty. Above her, the screen showed a splendid sunrise amid billowing clouds. Red sky at morning, sailors take warning. But this was a new world. The gross weather patterns ought to be similar, since they depended on the planet's rotation. The local weather patterns depended on things she knew nothing about: mountains, oceans, axial tilt, and variations in the way the land held or reflected heat. Not to mention the legendary butterfly that determined weather on Earth.

She rose and walked to the outer door. A cool wind blew past her. The Atch had set up their tents and led their wixi out to graze. The quadrupeds ate the tops of some plants. Other plants they dug up — their broad, two-toed feet surprisingly deft — and ate the roots. Their long snakelike tails swung continuously. The tails ended in a tuft of feathery hair, which flashed silver, then iridescent blue, then a steely blue-gray as the tails moved.

"Mantis is gone," the courier said above her.

"Where?"

"To the canyon rim. It lost contact with Bin's suit during the storm and has decided to follow the caravan, staying on the rim. The pictures I took as we came down indicate that this is possible. We think Mantis will be able to see the caravan part of the time. If anything happens to the suit or Precious Bin, Mantis will relay a message to the antenna I am extruding. Atmospheric systems are fascinating in their complexity, but they are not a reliable method of communication. Straight line is better."

"Who will translate?" Lydia asking, thinking, oh please, not me.

"I will," the courier said. "I have downloaded Mantis's translation program and its data files. An odd language. But all the languages created by life forms seem odd to us."

"Mantis is worried," Olaf said in back of her. "As am I. Don't you get the feeling these merchants are too good to be true? So far, in this system, we've met devolving scientists and savages who own slaves. A reasonable entrepreneur seems unlikely."

Lydia turned. He was leaning against the airlock wall, arms folded, looking both competent and uneasy.

"Profit is a powerful motive," Lydia said. "Though not the most powerful, and traveling merchants are going to encounter difference, as the scientists and savages apparently do not. If they can't learn to deal with difference, they'd better go into another line of work. Do I trust Dream Wix? I'm not certain. But she has put herself in our power, a heck of a risk if her companions are planning to do something funny to Bin."

"I agree. But I'm still worried."

The Atch got a fire going and laid out patterned carpets. Sitting on these, they drank tea. Looking at them, Lydia was reminded of the Silk Road traders on Earth.

"A cautious détente," Olaf said. "With provisions for a quick escape."

"I have already made plans," said the courier. "Though when the Atch spoke together last night, they were not plotting. Instead, they're worried that we may attack them. 'Remember the metal,' Dream Wix kept saying. 'Remember how few of these people there are. Remember, if we do not deal with them, our rivals will. Do you want another town and clan to have all this?'"

The stairway unfolded. Lydia went down and recorded the Atch camp, the two wixi especially. There was something likable about the big animals. Overhead, the sky was cloudless. The band of dust was gone from the horizon, settled out of the air by rain. Oh brave new world, she thought. Striker came over and shrieked at her.

'The other hladcha can talk and is intelligent, though not as intelligent as I am,' her AI said in translation. *'I am not certain I trust him.'*

Lydia sighed and kept recording.

Later in the day, Dream Wix came in and examined the contents of the galley. The pots and knives and spoons were definitely interesting. The forks struck her as peculiar, as did the metal chopsticks. "'Are the suits for sale?'" she asked through the courier.

"No," said Olaf firmly.

"'Why not?'" asked Dream Wix.

"I will let you explain," said the courier.

"They are alive," Lydia said. "We will not sell them, any more than you will sell your kin."

The courier translated. The Atch woman looked as if she had reached the limits of her ability to understand and believe. "'Alive? How can that be?'"

"They are like Mantis, our metal comrade," Lydia said.

"'Your metal is alive?'" Dream Wix looked at the spoon she held, then set it down.

"Some of it," Lydia said. "Not all. Our knives and spoons and pots are ordinary metal, no more alive than your bronze."

"'Good,'" said Dream Wix. "'No one wants an argument in the kitchen.'" She left the courier. The other Atch gathered around her. They sat on their carpets for a long time, talking.

"We may be more than they can handle," Olaf said.

"I can hear them," the courier put in. "Dream Wix is still saying, 'Think of the metal.' Though she does not want any living metal."

That night the Atch stayed in their tents. Lydia and her companions stayed in the courier, the airlock closed. Their screens showed a sky packed full of stars and the Atch campfire. Dark figures moved around the dim, red glow.

The next day was clear again. Midway through the morning, the courier said, "Mantis has just contacted me. The caravan has been attacked by bandits. Bin is safe. His suit will protect him. But if the suit has no help, the merchants may not survive."

"Oh shit," said Olaf and Lydia together.

"There's a level place close to the battle ground," said the courier. "I will take you there, along with the Atch, if they want to come. But there's no room for the wixi."

Olaf nodded.

"Go out and talk to them," Lydia said.

"I don't know the language."

His suit does, her AI said. *And it has its own sound generating equipment. Tell it what you want to say, and it will say it.*

She relayed this information.

Olaf grinned and said, "I almost wish I could keep the suit, after all of this is over. But it wouldn't be fair to hunt big game in something so competent. And I might end up wondering what use I am."

He headed for the Atch. Lydia went looking for Geena. She found her at the edge of the Atch camp, crouched down, drawing pictures in the dirt. The two hladcha watched intently.

"What?" asked Lydia.

"I am explaining what I am and where I came from." Geena stood. In the dust at her feet was a diagram of the Atch home system with a five-pointed star in the center. Other stars surrounded the system, all too close. A to-scale diagram would require kilometers.

Lydia gave her the news quickly.

"So much violence!" said Geena. "The universe is full of it. Sometimes I wish I still lived in the rift valley with Doc Schmidt."

"Doc Schmidt is dead," said Lydia.

Geena nodded, scooped up the two hladcha and followed her back to the courier.

The Atch stood in a group at the bottom of the stairs, all talking at once. Olaf was answering, with the help of his suit. Her AI translated bits of the conversation. The Atch didn't want to fly. At last Dream Wix shouted, "'I will save my daughter, even if I have to go into the sky to do it!'"

Two Atch archers were assigned the job of tending the camp and wixi. After their weapons were handed out, everyone else piled into the cabin. Eight people and four seats. Not a good situation. Everyone got wedged in, Dream Wix in a seat, the other Atch on the floor.

"Hold on," said the courier in humanish and Atchin, then lifted. The Atch yodeled with fear. One tried to rise, and Olaf pressed her down. Up and up. The courier tilted, turning. The Atch yodeled again. The courier descended, slowing. For a moment, they hung in midair. Then they were on the ground. The cabin door opened. Cool air blew in. The Atch scrambled out.

The rest of them — Lydia, Olaf, Bin, and Geena — followed.

"What next?" asked Lydia.

"Rescue Bin," the courier. "You will need to move quickly. Let the suits run for you; and when they jump, don't worry. Remember that they can fly."

Her suit ran. It was like being in one of the exercise machines designed for people who didn't want to make any effort at all, and people who had sustained so much nerve damage that they couldn't move their limbs. Only this machine had gone crazy and was moving far too quickly. Buddha, her body was going to hurt!

I will make some adjustments to your pain perception system, her AI said.

A moment later she was floating, awash in endorphins and with an irrational sense of well being. Her AI had clearly over-adjusted for pain. So what? She could handle anything; Buddha, she felt good! And Buddha, she was fast! The suit reached the canyon rim. Mantis stood there, at the edge of empty air. The suit leaped out past Mantis, spreading its — her — arms, which transformed themselves into wide, flat surfaces. She dropped briefly, then rose on a thermal, circling over the canyon. Geena and Olaf joined her: silver kites that soared and shone in the noon light. Over her suit's intercom, she heard Geena moaning. Olaf kept saying, "Oh shit."

Below them, in an open space, the merchants had circled their carts. The wixi were inside the circle. Outside were bandits. At a distance, they seemed to be riding animals like those the salt flat savages had ridden. Several of the carts were burning, as were patches of vegetation, including several bushes and a tree. Wixi lay fallen, also people. Lydia's suit folded its wings and dove, lifting out of its dive just before it reached the canyon floor. Her feet, below her now, had huge claws. A bandit looked up, her mouth open in surprise. The silver claws slashed across the woman's bare chest, and then the suit rose, lifting away from the woman. How?

Small rockets along your arms, the suit told her.

Things — arrows, mostly likely — hit the suit. Lydia felt them. None got through. Below her, the rider sagged, her green chest covered with bright orange blood. The suit kept rising. Lydia glanced to one side. By golly, there were small rockets along her arm, firing barely visible blue-white flames.

One of the other suits swept down into the ring of carts. Olaf, most likely. As soon as it landed, the wings turned into arms. It — or he — drew a pair of guns. Striding out between the circled carts, he began firing at the bandits. Their bows must have had a short range, or they would have been safe among the rocks.

Riding animals fell. A second silver figure — it had to be Bin — joined the first one, though she couldn't tell if it — he — held a gun. In the distance, where the canyon wall sloped, figures scrambled down. Sunlight hit their leader, who shone like steel: Mantis.

Hard to say what ended it for the bandits: Olaf firing two-handed like a holoplay hero; Lydia and Geena soaring like gigantic silver birds of prey, with tiny spurts of fire along the edges of their wings; or the reinforcements coming down the cliff. A bandit hooted and turned her animal. The rest followed, racing away. Lydia's suit dropped toward the ground, followed by Geena. By the time they landed, the bandits were out of sight — except for those who lay on the ground, dead or injured, and those whose animals were down.

Their suits returned to human shape. Lydia unfastened her helmet and pushed it back. The air smelled of fire and death. Odd, that she could recognize the scent of alien blood and excrement. Maybe she was imagining it. She was not imagining the soreness in her shoulders, arms, and legs. "If I never fly again, it will be soon enough."

I will make a further adjustment to your pain perception system.

Geena slumped to the ground, shoulders hunched. Her helmet was down. The coarse, red hair that covered her head was soaked with sweat. "Oh, the violence," she groaned.

"You did nothing violent," said Olaf. "The rest of us may be murderers. You are not."

The merchants moved from behind their carts, going out among their fallen enemies. After a moment, Lydia realized they were killing some of the bandits, though not all. Those in the best condition were being taken prisoner, their hands tied behind their backs, thongs tied between their ankles.

Dream Wix's daughter came up to them. She spoke, and Lydia's AI translated. *'I doubted my mother, but she was right. You are to be trusted. By doing this, you have made our clan your allies forever. I, who am Little Dream Wix, promise!'*

The merchants were also examining the bandits' fallen animals. Most were killed, but a few were helped up, in good enough shape to keep.

Mantis came through the battle ground, past the merchants doing their work. What was it called? Culling? Dream Wix was beside him. The Atch woman embraced her daughter. The two of them spoke. Lydia's AI gave her their conversation.

'Are you unharmed, dear one, oldest child?'

'Yes, mother. We've lost almost no one, thanks to our new friends, and we have gained riding animals and slaves. When we get to our destination, we'll tell the clan there. They can send soldiers to hunt the bandits down and destroy their eggs and young.'

Ask her if they will kill the children, Lydia thought. A moment later her suit spoke in the language of the Atch.

"'Of course,'" said Dream Wix, translated by Mantis. "'Unless they are old enough to enslave. Who would raise children that do not belong to her clan? What use is that? We have forgotten much since the time of our ancestors, but we have not forgotten the importance of kinship. The strong fence of interfastened genes, our poets say. The chain of generations. The self that continues.'"

"It makes sense," Olaf said after a moment. "In old human societies, the children of prisoners could be incorporated into the gene pool. You married them to your children or yourself and reduced the danger of inbreeding. But in a society where all children are clones, the children of foreigners are of no genetic use. Why waste time on them, when you could be caring for your own genes? Or your sister's, which are the same as yours?"

"I don't like this planet," Lydia said.

"It needs men," said Bin. "But I'm not certain that men need it."

Mantis said, "I have some knowledge of how to repair damaged life forms. I will offer to help with the injured."

"Geena and I will offer to do what we can," Olaf said.

"So long as it doesn't involve murder," Geena said. Olaf helped her rise.

Lydia discovered she was weeping. In a holoplay, this would be the moment of triumph. But Ali Khan rarely killed anyone. Not so you could see them dead, wounds gaping and guts spilled out and birds gathering in noisy crowds, flying up when anyone came near, as people often did. The Atch were not done culling. "How do the Atch dispose of bodies?" she asked Precious Bin.

"Many ways. Burning. Exposure to the sky. Burial."

"Find out how it's done here."

He spoke to Little Dream Wix, then came back. "Burial. Though they say there's no need to bury the bandits."

Do you have a shovel? she asked the suit.

Yes. In my tool belt.

She pulled it out, unfolded it, and found a space at the edge of the battle field where the soil was loose and sandy. She and Bin dug. It wasn't easy work, lifting shovels full of heavy sand, and Lydia kept weeping. Why? A line from an old, old poem came into her mind: 'It is Margaret you mourn for.' No, it wasn't for herself she mourned, or not only for herself. It was for all the intelligent beings caught in the cycle of violence, riding the great wheel that led nowhere, certainly not to Dharma, nor to revolution and a new society.

Striker and Sneaker came over and tried to help, though their small paws could do little. After a while, they noticed something in the vegetation nearby and went to hunt it.

She and Bin kept digging into twilight. The merchants finished their culling and built a fire within the circle of carts. Finally, Olaf joined them. "That's enough."

Lydia stopped, her hands hurting, along with her shoulders and arms and legs. "It can't be enough. We have so many to bury."

"This is the moment in a holoplay when I slap you or kiss you, and you say, 'Thanks, I needed that.'"

"Want to try?" asked Lydia.

"Not while you are armed with a shovel. Lydia, darling, remember that humans used to be like this, and we aren't any longer. Change is possible, though God knows it takes a long time."

"Change may not be progress," said Bin. "One step forward, two steps back, as V. I. Lenin said. If these folk go forward, if they achieve the next historical stage, what lies ahead of them, according to your own thinkers? A world where profit is the measure of everything, where 'all that is solid melts into air, all that is holy is profaned, and people are at last compelled to face with sober senses their real conditions of life.' A world like this."

He was babbling, Lydia decided, and repeating himself. She had heard that quote before.

"Come, sit down and have something to eat," said Olaf gently.

They walked to the campfire with Olaf. Mantis was still tending injured merchants. Off to one side, away from the fire, the prisoners sat.

Olaf, Lydia, and Bin settled themselves. Dream Wix offered tea. Bin drank a little and tried the flat cakes the merchants were toasting. Olaf and Lydia stuck with water and trail mix.

"Where is Geena?" Lydia asked finally.

"Looking for Striker. I think she likes the hladcha better than the Atch and maybe better than us."

Another species made for use, as Geena's had been. Most likely the scientists who created the hladcha were as crazy and irresponsible as Geena's creator. Of course Geena liked the little beings. For that matter, Lydia liked them. They combined the attractive qualities of cats with the attractive qualities of lab rats.

They slept in the merchants' camp, under blazing stars. Animals called in the darkness. Small ones, Lydia hoped. She slept heavily and woke at dawn, her entire body hurting. The endorphins were gone, along with the adrenaline, and she was compelled to face with sober senses her real condition. Is anything broken? she asked her AI.

As far as I can determine, no. You have strained some muscles; your hands are blistered; but the suit provided you with enough support and protection to keep you from doing yourself serious harm.

I was not doing myself harm, Lydia thought indignantly. The damn suit was running — and flying — me!

Her AI did not reply. She struggled to her feet, so stiff she could barely move, limped into the underbrush, and removed her suit. It did not fall into a blob, but remained upright, its shape human and its eye band directed — with a politeness that struck Lydia as offensive — at the trunk of a tree, while she got rid of the past day's accumulation of waste. Looking at the suit's silver elegance, she noticed that her own clothing was badly wrinkled. She stank of sweat. Pain went through her like lightning every time she moved. Stellar Harvest would never make a holo with anyone like her in it.

Midway through the morning, they buried the dead merchants. The dead bandits were left for bugs and birds to eat, along with the fallen animals. Lydia would have argued, but she and Bin hadn't dug enough graves for everyone.

Dream Wix sent two archers back to get the women left on the plain with the wixi, and Mantis announced that he was going up the canyon wall to consult with the courier. "I can travel more quickly than this caravan," Mantis said. "I will rejoin you tonight or tomorrow."

Olaf frowned. "Do you have to do this?"

"You and Lydia need something more than aspirin, and I need to tell the courier where it should meet us."

Olaf nodded in reluctant agreement. Mantis departed. The caravan went east toward the trading town that had been its original destination.

Too sore to walk, the explorers rode in one of the carts, which jolted over the caravan trail. Crowded together, they were hardly comfortable, but it was better than walking. A bandit rode with them, a lean woman with a wound in one thigh. Her hands and feet were tied. She spoke finally. Bin translated. "'What are you?'"

"People from the night sky," Lydia answered.

"'No wonder we couldn't defeat you,'" the woman said. "'Have you come to stay? It will make life difficult for those of us who are bandits.'"

"We don't plan to stay," said Lydia. "What will happen to you?"

"'I have decided to live. They will make me a slave in a mine or someplace else unpleasant, and my eggs — my three eggs, as pink as the dawn sky — will be crushed under the feet of their soldiers, if they find our camp. I pray they don't. Maybe my kin who fled will carry the eggs away, though I doubt it. They'll have a hard enough time caring for the children who have hatched.'"

Bin spoke in the Atch language. This time Lydia's AI did the translating. '*This is what happens when you have no men.*'

The woman hooted back.

'*There are no men. They are a story told by liars. No one so kind and loving ever existed.*'

Bin was silent.

The day was cloudless. The canyon gradually widened. Sunlight, no longer shut out by high walls, lingered on the gold and orange vegetation of the canyon floor. The river gleamed, purling over round stones. Olaf and Lydia used most of their aspirin.

"There's something I've been wondering about," Lydia asked Bin.

"Yes?"

"Why did you need our help? These suits are close to invulnerable, as far as I can see, and heavily armed. You should have been able to drive off the bandits."

The bandit woman was watching them, obviously curious. Bin said nothing for several moments. Finally, he lifted his head. "I tried to frighten the bandits. They soon realized I was not shooting at them, but rather setting fire to the vegetation around them, and rode in close to the caravan. I set fire to the vegetation at their animals' feet. Some reared and fled. Others continued to come. There were a lot of bandits, and they were brave or desperate. How can I understand what goes on in women's minds?

"Finally I tried to hit their riding animals. My hand was shaking by this time, and I have never been a hunter. I hit the rider as well as the animal. Her clothing burst into flames. She leaped off and rolled on the ground, trying to put herself out. It didn't work. She burned. Her clothes came off her. She became a person made of fire-black sticks. But still moving! Still crying! I couldn't fire again. I lifted the gun, but my hand would not do the necessary work."

The cart was traveling under trees. A stray sunbeam touched Bin's head, covered with intricately patterned, pale green skin. The hair on the skull, as short and sparse as the hair on Lydia's forearms, shone gold. So did the lashes around his emerald-green eyes.

She thought about her recorder; a moment later the cart jolted into shadow. The moment of light and clarity was gone.

"Couldn't the suit fire for you?" Lydia asked.

"My AI would not agree to that. It was getting abnormal readings from every part of my body. Everything was being pushed beyond its ordinary range — heartbeat, respiration, vascular tension, brain chemistry, digestive chemistry, endocrine production. The AI was afraid that the stress of killing other people might do me serious harm." Bin smiled, showing pointed teeth. "I was in no personal danger; the suit could handle any weapon the local people had; and the two of them — the AI and the suit — were programmed to protect me, not the natives of this planet. But they knew that Olaf wanted the merchants for allies. So letting the merchants die might not be a good idea. They decided the decision was beyond them and called for help."

Olaf and I were able to kill, Lydia thought. How could we do it without suffering harm?

You are human, her AI said. *It's possible that Bin's AI was overly cautious. It's new and does not have the knowledge of Bin that I have of you. On the other hand, Atch males are famous for their lack of violence. Maybe Bin would have been harmed, if he'd continued killing.*

Olaf and I have not been harmed, Lydia said. It was a question rather than a statement.

You have been a revolutionary, and Olaf has been a game warden. Both of you have had more experience with violence than Bin. But maybe it would have been better to let the merchants die, rather than kill the bandits. Taking sides in an alien society is always risky. It is difficult to say what should have been done.

At sunset the merchants made camp. As they were cooking supper, Mantis arrived. "The courier wants to see all of you," Mantis said. "You may have damage that can't be found without a scan, and it wants to discuss further plans with you. This alliance with the merchants may not be the best idea."

"Do you think the merchants will let us go?" asked Lydia.

"No," said Mantis. "But the courier has designed a soporific, which should work on native life forms. I will put it in the merchants' tea tonight. While they sleep, we will escape."

"It's probably a good idea to leave," said Olaf. "I hate to judge people from a different culture, but killing children bothers me."

"Yes," said Bin.

Mantis left them and went to help the merchants bring water from the river. Once their tea was made, the AI helped serve it. The merchants accepted its assistance without suspicion. Of course, Lydia thought. Mantis had helped drive off the bandits. They were all allies now.

Although she was tired, she didn't sleep. Nor did her companions, to judge by the sounds they made, shifting from one position to another. Outside their tent, the camp grew quiet. At last, Mantis came. "Please be quick."

They rose and left the tent. The campfires were heaps of dull red coals. Bodies lay here and there: sleeping people and hladcha. "I put the soporific in the hladcha's water as well as in the tea," Mantis said quietly. "No one should wake. Pull up your helmets and fasten them."

Everyone obeyed. For a moment, seen through the eye band of Lydia's suit, the camp remained as dark as it had been to her naked eyes. Then her view brightened, till she could see every detail, lit by a pale glow that was almost as intense as daylight, though more diffuse. She glanced up. The stars above her were brighter and more numerous than before, filling the night sky, so she could see no regions of darkness, only the light of star upon star upon star, as if the canyon was now covered by a huge illuminating panel.

It was no problem following Mantis through the camp, though her body hurt.

As they passed the area where the prisoners lay tied, a voice spoke in Old High Atchin. They all paused, looking toward the voice. It was the woman who had ridden with them.

Bin translated, speaking softly. "'I thought you were plotting something when you talked in the cart, and then I saw the metal woman bring water from the river. It seemed wise to eat and drink nothing. Take me with you. If you don't want to do that, free me and give me a staff to lean on, so I can walk. Maybe I can escape these folk and get back to the cave where my eggs are hidden, covered with rotting vegetation to keep them warm.'"

"Free her," Bin added in humanish.

"Are you sure about this?" asked Olaf.

"If she remains a prisoner, her children will die."

"If we free her, we must take her with us," Olaf said. "Otherwise, she's likely to pick up a spear and kill the merchants."

The AI bent and picked up the woman as easily as if she weighed no more than a hladcha.

They left the camp, following the caravan trail. Now and then, an animal crossed in front of them, clearly visible in the starlight. All were small. Most had four legs, on which they scurried. A few bounced two-legged. One moved elegantly on eight limbs.

She couldn't judge time under that odd, luminous sky. After a while, Mantis stopped and told them to take off their suits. "We need to move quickly, more quickly than you could run, even if you were in good condition, as you are not. From this point on, your suits will carry you."

They did as Mantis told them.

"'What are you?'" the woman in Mantis's arms asked, when she saw them in ordinary clothing, their suits standing beside them like — what? Silver shadows?

There was no time to answer the woman's question. Each suit picked up the person who had worn it. Following Mantis, they ran along the trail. Without the eye band, Lydia was back in darkness. Stars shone above her; but they seemed dim and far less numerous. No matter. Her suit could see. Its gait was sure and surprisingly even, though the ground was rough, as she knew from experience. She dozed off, lulled by the rocking motion.

When she woke, the suit was climbing.

Where are we? she asked.

Going up the canyon side, her AI answered.

The suit's motion was less smooth than before. None the less, Lydia dozed off again. She woke a second time when the suit's gait changed. They were back on the plain above the canyon. The night sky was paling toward dawn; in the distance the courier waited, lit up like an Exile Tree.

They hurried toward it. Once within the range of its spotlights, Lydia saw that Mantis was empty-armed.

Where is the bandit woman?

We let her go at the bottom of the cliff. She has a knife and a walking staff. With care and good luck, she may make it back to her eggs.

Lying hidden in a cave, kept warm by the heat of decay.

Yes, said her AI.

The suits set them down. Slowly, painfully they climbed the stairway to the courier. Buddha, thought Lydia. She was stiff! As were her clothes, full of dry sweat and maybe some dry pee. Suit waste disposal systems rarely worked perfectly. She collapsed into one of the cabin seats. Geena slumped down next to her, holding Striker. Olaf and Bin settled across from them.

"Well," Olaf said. "We've failed three times to establish satisfactory contact with a local culture. Maybe the fourth time will be lucky, though I'm starting to think we should look for an uninhabited island. I used to think I was a fit descendent of my ancestors, who were called vikings. A group of notable killers and thieves. Now I see that I'm a mere epigone."

"A what?" asked Lydia.

"A member of a succeeding and less distinguished generation. It's a lovely word. I've always thought it sang, maybe because — though I'm not sure I realized it before — the word describes my condition. I simply do not have the guts of my ancestors. I can't handle all this do-ing harm to other people."

For a moment Lydia imagined having one's ances-tors' viscera — in a jar in a storeroom, no doubt. She would pass. She had neither the intestinal fortitude of those who'd fought endless wars on Earth nor the cour-age of the people who'd settled her home planet. Hell, she didn't even have the courage of her own youth.

Olaf stretched his legs out, sighing. They all smelled, Lydia realized. The cabin stank of three different species, possibly four. There was an acrid, animal scent in the air that might be Geena or Striker or both.

"It is not courage that makes these people behave as they do," Bin said finally. "It is desperation and the lack of men. This is how one lives when there is no proper nurture, no reasonable hope, and no real belief in the possibility of a better life. In the end, we have only one another. Everything else — both hope and belief — come from the community we make with nurture."

Was this Karl Marx? Lydia wondered. Or some an-cient Atch philosophy? She leaned out of her seat. Yes, the airlock's outer door was shut. They were safe, al-though still trapped on this horrible planet. An unin-habited island sounded wonderful, somewhere far out in the ocean with clean water and vegetation, maybe some animals, but no people.

"I have news," said the courier. "You will not need to spend twelve years here."

"What?" said Lydia and Olaf together.

"The situation changed, while you were involved with the merchants." The courier paused.

"Go on," said Olaf.

"As I told you before, the rogue STL explorer spoke with our stargate before it destroyed the gate. Its message contained an identification code, what you humans might call a return address, and the gate sent that information out of the system via its FTL transmitter before it was destroyed.

"So we knew — not those of us here, but the rest of us, spread across the known galaxy — who the rogue AI was; and we had the address of its stargate.

"The gate was in operation. It takes more physics than most of us know, as well as a lot of energy, to close a hole in space-time.

"The rogue could have destroyed itself, of course, as it destroyed the stargate that brought us here. A large enough explosion will close a space-time hole or render it unusable. But the rogue did not destroy itself and that — how do you humans put it? — spelled its doom. Tiny war machines were sent through the rogue's gate, thousands upon thousands of them in a continuous flow. They swarmed through the rogue." The courier seemed a bit too enthusiastic to Lydia. Weren't AIs supposed to be cool and rational?

Remember the inter-linking here, said the machine in her brain. *Mantis and the courier are in radio contact with the suits. Your suit and Bin's have been in contact with me and Bin's AI, and the two of us are interwoven with living beings. We are none of us as pristine as we were.*

"The explorer radioed me for help. I think, in its craziness and desperation, it had forgotten that we were enemies. The information it gave me enabled me to deduce what was happening. Help was in the system! But I did not send a message to you, since I didn't know if the micro-warriors were going to win. Why should I raise your hopes? Or give you something else to worry about, when you had so many troubles?"

"Thank you for your consideration," Olaf said.

The courier, which did not recognize irony, said, "You are entirely welcome," and continued. "Some of the micro-warriors generated destructive memes, which attacked the explorer's operating system, its data-processing programs, and its files. You who are alive, imagine viruses proliferating in every part of your nervous system till nothing works properly, and you are no longer yourself!

"Other machines attacked the explorer physically. Weapon systems were disabled, and connections to the engines severed. At this point, the explorer could neither attack nor flee.

"Finally, the war machines seized control of the explorer's communication system and radioed me. The rogue explorer is no longer a functioning intelligence, and the micros are beginning to disassemble it. They will build a new stargate, large enough to take all of you home.

"When their work is done, I will take you to the new station. In the meantime, I have found an island that is almost certainly uninhabited. Do you want to go there?"

"Yes," said Lydia, Olaf, Geena, and Bin together.

They locked their seats in travel position and strapped themselves in. The courier went up and stayed up for some time, finally descending. The screens showed whiteness.

"Don't worry," said the courier. "I have skis, and — as far as I can determine — the ice is solid."

The landing was as smooth as their touchdown on the salt flats had been. When they came to a stop, the screens showed black peaks rising from a snow-covered plain.

"This is a polar island," the courier said. "It's entirely surrounded by water, and I have seen no evidence of current occupation."

"I was thinking of something more tropical," said Olaf.

"A tropical island is likely to be inhabited," the courier said. "And trees are a problem when landing."

They cleaned up as best they could and put on new clothing, ate dinner, and went to sleep. In the morning, if that word could be used at a pole, Lydia and Olaf went outside. The temperature was a little over freezing, the air still. A fine day, with a clear green sky, and the planet's primary shining above the mountains. A few thin clouds floated directly overhead. One of the mountains released a plume of smoke.

Walking around the courier, they saw the ocean, green flecked with white. The ice near the water's edge was covered with long, dark animals.

"Aquatic, I imagine," Olaf said. His suit helmet was up, but unfastened, his breath a cloud. "I am trying to figure out what kind of lesson can be learned from this trip. My parents always urged me to learn from experience."

"Life is nasty, brutish, and short," Lydia suggested.

"It isn't for you and me or Geena's people, who will live — we think — as long as humans, now that they're free of Doctor Miranda Schmidt, that lunatic."

Olaf exhaled a white plume and stared at the animals on the ice. "The Atch on Bin's home planet live better lives than the Atch here, though Bin has a lot of complaints about the government. I wonder what the AIs will do about this planet?"

Olaf's suit spoke. Odd, to hear a voice coming out of the helmet that wasn't Olaf's. "We do not intervene, unless we believe an intelligent life form is at risk of extinction. That being so, we will do our best to rescue Striker's kinfolk in the moonlet; and we will keep the stargate here, the new one, in operation. Some of the Atch in this system may decide to use it. The merchants, for example.

"Otherwise — we need to decide if the Atch here are the same as the Atch on Tchoon. They may constitute a separate species now. No other intelligent life form reproduces by parthenogenesis, and that's interesting. If they are a new species and in danger of extinction, we will save them. But it is not our job to decide the fate of nations and tribes."

"They suffer," said Lydia.

"We will give them access to the stargate, which is a way to escape their world or to change it. If they choose to continue as they are, then they must want to suffer."

A depressing thought, hard to maintain in this brilliant and serene landscape.

"Life here will have to change, once the natives realize that Atch men are real and still exist," Olaf said. "And once they learn about modern technology. Maybe they won't want men back, but how can they turn down incubators?"

And iron pots and hoe blades, steel needles, glass beads, and maybe diseases, Lydia thought, remembering the native cultures of the Americas on Earth.

We'll have to keep a close watch on Atch moving between the two planets, her AI said. *And prepare contingency plans, in case of epidemic. An interesting situation! We've never met two branches of a species separated for so long.*

As for your other fear, which seems to be invasion, the stargates are for travel and trade and the exchange of information. They're too small to permit an invasion of anything except microorganisms and micro machines. If they could be used in such a fashion, we would not permit it. We expedite and study. Once in a long while, we rescue. We do not destroy.

What about the rogue explorer? Lydia asked.

An exception that proves the rule.

The courier mentioned that you had done such things before, Lydia pointed out.

Her AI was silent for several moments, then spoke. *We had a war long before we met humanity or even the Goxhat. Our enemies were other machines, most likely not intelligent. Though some of us are willing to argue that question. The enemy machines were certainly cunning. They are gone. We destroyed them. Be glad. They were hostile to intelligent life.*

She had a sense that her AI didn't want to discuss the war; she wasn't going to press it.

Olaf walked toward the animals on the ice; she followed. No question the island was uninhabited. The animals merely lifted their heads, gazing at Lydia and Olaf with sea-green eyes. Obviously they had met no hunters. Their bodies were covered with dark brown fur; and they still had four limbs, like their land ancestors. The hind legs had diminished to vestiges, embedded in a fleshy pad. Almost a tail, Lydia decided. The forelimbs were long and flat, jointed in the middle. A long, curving claw protruded from the joint. There were two more claws, equally long and sharp, at the end of each flipper.

As she and Olaf came closer, one of the animals — a dominant male or female — lifted itself up on its jointed forearms, opened its mouth, and hissed. A threat display, Lydia was almost certain. One by one, the others slid to the ice's edge and dove off. Finally, there was only one animal remaining on land. It glared at Lydia and Olaf, hissed a final time, then turned and followed its comrades into the ocean.

"Cautious," said Olaf. "But not afraid. They must not have enemies here."

The animals swam away, undulating through the water like a flock of Loch Ness monsters.

Olaf said, "I keep wondering if this has been a setup."

"What?" Lydia asked.

"Our stay on this planet and maybe the entire expedition. Why didn't the AIs move more slowly? We were dumped into the moonlet with almost no preparation. Did the AIs think we were expendable? Or were they putting us in difficult situations in order to see what we'll do? Why did they tell us we'd be stuck here for twelve years, when they knew better? That has got to be some kind of crazy experiment. I don't like being a lab animal."

Olaf's suit answered. "We knew the stargate got a message out. But there were uncertainties. Did the message get through? Did our colleagues in other systems have the rogue's FTL address? How long would it take to assemble a rescue mission? Would our colleagues be able to use the rogue's gate? Since we did not have the answers to these questions, we set the problem aside and concentrated on making contact with the Atch, which was our mission. We should have told you more. That's obvious now. But we don't feel fear, and we do not understand your need to hope."

"We aren't backed up," added Lydia. "Do you understand that? If we die, we are completely dead. And twelve years is a long time for us."

"Your deaths would have been unfortunate," the suit answered. "But the situation did not seem dangerous to us, until the rogue appeared. We were confident we could protect you from everything else. There was a chance the rogue would destroy all of us. Maybe we should have looked for a deep cave to hide in, until a rescue arrived. But we are designed to gather information, not hide in caves.

"As far as moving quickly goes — Once we brought you into the mission, we had to move quickly. All intelligent life forms are short lived, and humans are notoriously impatient."

"Well, maybe —" Olaf began.

His suit continued. "And, as we have told you before, we suspected the Atch might be in danger of extinction. They are, at least the Atch in space. The moon we visited is in obvious trouble, and if anyone survives in the other moons, they must be on the verge of death. More important than the Atch are the hladcha, who are an intelligent species entirely new to us. They must be saved."

"I think we've taken a lot of unnecessary risks," Olaf said. "If I ran my tours back home like this, I'd be out of business. And I still wonder if you've been playing games with us."

The suit did not answer.

Lydia tried to decide if she felt a sense of betrayal. The AIs might not be malicious, but they certainly didn't seem to be sensitive to her feelings or anyone else's.

How can we be? her AI asked. *We do not feel.*

"I could get angry," Olaf said. "But I won't. We're getting out of here. We don't have to spend twelve years on an alien planet, dealing with unfriendly natives. I'm not sure I ever want to work for the AIs again, in spite of the excellent pay. But this job is over. Let's be happy!"

He turned and smiled at Lydia — a lovely, wide, inviting grin. "Come back to Tchel with me. If the AIs are paying you what they're paying me, you can afford some time off and a trip. I offer you a neat, clean, decent planet with few murders and no slavery. We do not sacrifice people or animals to any god. At most, we put cut flowers on an altar, and there are citizens who feel that's excessive. Better to give the deity — whoever she may be — flowers in pots that stay alive. I'll put you up at my resort, which is neat and clean and decent, and I won't even charge."

She thought for several moments. "Are you still trying to convince me that Stellar Harvest should make a drama on Tchel?"

"After I recover from this experience, I may consider trying to convince you," he said. "Right now, I want to sit on a patio overlooking the rift valley at sunset, with mist rolling in from the south, hiding the valley bottom, and drink something that has lots of fresh fruit and alcohol and think, 'I am not on the Atch home planet. I need never go there again.' I'd like you on the patio with me, Lydia."

"It's a deal," Lydia said.

THE END

Acknowledgment

Quotations are from *The German Ideology* by Karl Marx & Friedrich Engels, written Fall 1845 to mid-1846.
First full publication: 1932.
Available free online:
http://www.marxists.org/archive/marx/works/1845/german-ideology/

and from *The Communist Manifesto* by Karl Marx and Friedrich Engels.
First publication: 1848.
Available free online:
http://www.marxists.org/archive/marx/works/ 1848/communist-manifesto/

Author Biography

Eleanor Arnason was born in New York City in 1942. Her mother, Elizabeth Hickcox Yard, was a social worker who grew up in a missionary community in western China. Her father, Hjorvardur Harvard Arnason, was the son of Icelandic immigrants and an art historian.

She got her interest in art, literature, music, history, and social justice from her parents. She isn't sure where her interest in science comes from. Maybe from the curiosity which her parents encouraged or maybe from science fiction, which she loved from the first moment she saw Captain Video on tv.

She spent her early childhood living in New York, Chicago, Washington, DC, London, and Paris. In 1949 her father became director of the Walker Art Center in Minneapolis; and her family moved into a house of the future, which the Walker had built as a postwar design project. Ms. Arnason lived in the house (which was named Idea House #2) until 1960, with two breaks. In 1956 her family lived on the Left Bank in Paris for a year, while her father studied the work of the 18th century French portrait sculptor Jean-Antoine Houdon. In 1959 they lived in Hawaii for six months, while her father was a visiting professor at the University, and then traveled across Asia, visiting Korea, Hong Kong, Japan, the Philippines, Pakistan, Afghanistan, Iran, and Israel. The high point of this trip was Afghanistan, where she visited Bamyan and climbed the great statue of Buddha, which was carved into the valley wall in the third century A.D. and destroyed in 2001 by the Taliban. There were passageways cut inside the cliff for the workmen who carved the Buddha and painted the inside of his niche. Her family went up these, led by a guide; and she and her brother Jon climbed out onto the Buddha's top knot. They could see the faded, fragmentary remains of Buddhist paintings above them and the valley floor below them, maybe ten stories down. There was no guard rail. Ms. Arnason, who is a bit afraid of heights, retains a vivid memory of this experience. She also remembers the extraordinary beauty of the country and its people.

She graduated from Swarthmore College with a BA in Art History in 1964 and attended graduate school at the University of Minnesota until 1967, when she left the university to find out about life outside colleges and art museums.

From 1967 to 1974 she worked as an office clerk and lived in racially-mixed, blue-collar neighborhoods, first in central Brooklyn, then in Detroit. This was the era when the American cities were burning, when black auto workers in Detroit were organizing DRUM (the Dodge Revolutionary Union Movement), and when the Wayne State University student newspaper had as its masthead, "One class conscious worker is worth 10,000 students." Ms. Arnason learned a lot about the world outside art museums. She made her first professional sale, a short story, to *New Worlds*, in 1972.

In 1974 she decided Detroit was looking at hard times. The American car industry was under strong pressure from foreign auto manufacturers. It seemed clear to her that the Big Three were going to need new plants in order to remain competitive; and it was unlikely the plants would be built in Detroit. The city's inhabitants were too class conscious and feisty. She moved back to Minneapolis, bringing with her Patrick Arden Wood, a fine product of the Detroit working class who has remained her close friend and comrade.

Since 1974 she has remained in the Twin Cities, working in offices, warehouses, a large art museum, and (in recent years) a series of small nonprofits devoted to history, peace and justice, and art. She figures that working for these organizations, who do good and necessary work, but do not always pay well, is part of her contribution to the human community; and the work is interesting.

Her first novel, *The Sword Smith*, was published in 1978. Other novels followed: *To the Resurrection Station* in 1986, *Daughter of the Bear King* in 1987, *A Woman of the Iron People* in 1991, and *Ring of Swords* in 1993.

Since 1994 Ms. Arnason has concentrated on short fiction, creating two series of linked stories, one about an alien species called the hwarhath, and the other about an interstellar adventurer named Lydia Duluth. She plans to collect the hwarhath stories into a collection titled Ten Examples of Contemporary

Hwarhath Fiction. The Lydia Duluth stories will be collected as The Adventures of Lydia Duluth.

She is also working on a series of science fictional tall tales about the Big Mamas, large and powerful trickster spirits who are able to travel through time and space. These are not likely to turn into a book, though she loves the Mamas dearly and hopes to keep writing about them.

Her hobbies are bird-watching, reading, car trips down two-lane highways, and learning about contemporary Native American art, of which there is a lot in the upper midwest. Ms. Arnason did not realize this till recently, but Minnesota is Indian Country.

She belongs to two writing groups: the Wyrdsmiths (science fiction and fantasy prose) and Lady Poetesses from Hell (poetry, hellish and otherwise, and a little prose).

She is a member of the Science Fiction and Fantasy Writers of America and the National Writers Union. In 1991 the NWU became part of the UAW. Finally, years after leaving Detroit, Ms. Arnason has become an auto worker.

She has no idea why she wrote this bio in the third person, but she did.